Her lips were a straight path down from mine—

—and only inches away. For a split second I felt myself falling toward her. The movement was slight, but it made me dizzy and shaky like no other ride had that day.

Suddenly, just as I could feel my breath mixing with hers, I stopped and pulled back. It was like my sanity broke through my clouds of emotion. *What do you think you're doing, Foster?* I thought. *You can't kiss her! It's totally off-limits.*

I sat there, frozen, trying to sort out my senses. My heart felt like a battering ram inside my chest and my stomach seemed to be doing calisthenics. I had never flipped out like this before. What the heck was going on?

Love Stories

The "L" Word

Lynn Mason

BANTAM BOOKS
NEW YORK • TORONTO • LONDON • SYDNEY • AUCKLAND

To Christy McCartney Malan

RL 6, age 12 and up

THE "L" WORD
A Bantam Book / December 1998

Produced by 17th Street Productions,
a division of Daniel Weiss Associates, Inc.
33 West 17th Street
New York, NY 10011.
Cover photography by Michael Segal.

ISBN: 0-553-49249-7

Published simultaneously in the United States and Canada

Bantam Books are published by Bantam Books, a division of Bantam Doubleday Dell Publishing Group, Inc. Its trademark, consisting of the words "Bantam Books" and the portrayal of a rooster, is Registered in U.S. Patent and Trademark Office and in other countries. Marca Registrada. Bantam Books, 1540 Broadway, New York, New York 10036.

PRINTED IN THE UNITED STATES OF AMERICA

OPM 0 9 8 7 6 5 4 3 2 1

One

Sean

I KNEW I wasn't the first guy to have a girl break up with him. There were guys at school who'd been dumped, and I'd seen it on TV several times. I just never thought it would happen to me.

". . . nineteen . . . twenty . . . twenty-one . . . ," I grunted as I lifted the thirty-pound dumbbell. Lately my pent-up anger seemed to be a limitless source of strength. Here it was a lazy Saturday afternoon, a couple of weeks before Christmas break, and the only thing I could concentrate on was pumping iron.

When Jo Beth gave me the "I want to be friends" speech two weeks earlier, I just about lost it. It wasn't like I couldn't live without her—I'm not a weepy mama's boy or anything—but I felt like I'd been made a fool of. Let's face it: Whenever you hear about someone getting dumped, you always wonder what it is that made them so unacceptable. Bad breath? Lame personality? I imagined the students of Saddle Pass High School circulating their own theories, saying stuff like, "I hear Sean kisses like a largemouth bass," or, "He always put football before Jo Beth."

Plus the way she broke up with me was totally bogus. It was right after the pep rally for the last game of the season. I was all fired up to slaughter the Messina Mustangs. It was my last game as the Fightin' Pirates' star wide receiver. After two winning seasons with the team and several still talked-about plays, I had college scouts from all over giving me their cards. That night some dude from Florida State—my top choice for college—was going to be there.

All week long I'd been concentrating on the win. Working out. Eating right. Getting to bed early. Jo didn't like it that I wouldn't talk late on the phone with her or hang out at Willie's Chili (I didn't want to be tempted by the cheese fries), but I figured she knew how much the game meant to me and that I had to be in top condition.

Anyway, during the pep rally I was in major "game mode." I kept picturing the football descending like a guided missile into my hands, the stands quaking with cheering spectators, the talent-scout guy calling his boss on a cellular. I couldn't really concentrate on the skit Jo Beth and the rest of the squad were performing—the advanced art class had made a big papier-mâché horse, and the cheerleaders took turns trying to rope it. It was sort of lame, but the crowd got into it.

Afterward, when everyone was leaving, Jo stopped me. She pulled me back onto the gym floor and said she needed to talk. I was trying to stay in my focus zone and was barely paying attention to her. But when she said, "You know, Sean, it seems like we've grown apart," I snapped out of it.

I was so blown away, I didn't know what to do. I wanted to hit something. When I turned, the first thing I saw was the grinning face of that giant spit-wad horse. One punch snapped the head right off.

Later, during the game, I couldn't concentrate. I kept dropping the ball. Finally midway through the third quarter I made a rare catch on a crossing pattern. I had to stretch out to grab the ball, and before I could safely tuck it away, the middle linebacker's shoulder and helmet crashed into my midsection, jarring the ball loose. I tried to dive for it but got sandwiched by the cornerback and free safety, severely spraining my left knee. They recovered the fumble. I was out for the rest of the game.

The good news was the doc said I didn't need surgery and would heal up after a month or so. The bad news was Mr. Florida State hit the road without even saying good-bye.

The next couple of weeks I laid low at school.

I was kind of freaked by everything that went down. It reminded me of that weird book they made us read in English class—the one where the dude wakes up and realizes he's turned into a bug. I mean, I knew I wasn't a cockroach or anything, but I suddenly wasn't the person I thought I was. Before Jo Beth broke things off, I was Sean Foster, superjock, the guy with the cool girlfriend and promising athletic career. But suddenly I was starting to doubt everything about me.

" . . . twenty-six . . . twenty-seven . . ."

"Hey, Schwarzenegger." My little sister breezed into my room. "You going to Charlie Hornbeck's party tonight?"

"No," I said without looking up.

"Aw, come on. Everyone's going to be there. You'll have a blast."

"I said I wasn't going. Now get out of here. Can't you see I'm busy?" Claire didn't care about me having fun; she just knew that Dad would only let her go if I went. Usually I liked having her tag along to parties with me and Jo. That way I could keep an eye on the other jocks in case they got any ideas. Claire's real pretty, but she's only a freshman and still kind of naive. This time, though, she was out of luck. No way I was going to show up with my kid sister after just getting dumped.

"What's your deal anyway?" Claire stood right in front of me with her arms folded and a defiant frown on her face, like a freckle-faced rap artist.

"I mean it, Sean. For the past two weeks you've just been moping around like a stray dog. Either fall belly-up and die already or snap out of it."

"Hey, who asked your opinion? Get out of here and go nag someone else."

Claire sat down on my bed as if she hadn't heard me. "You know, I'm sorry Jo broke your heart and all, but you're only punishing yourself by acting this way."

"Give it a rest, Claire. What do you think this is? Some movie? *Sleepless in Saddle Pass*? I'm not asking for any advice. I'm telling you to get out of my face."

"But if you went out with your friends tonight, it would—"

"Get—"

"I mean, what are you so afraid of?"

"—out!" I was so mad, I bet my eyes were glowing red.

"Okay, okay. I'm going." Claire threw her arms up in the air and walked out. Just as she was closing the door she stuck her head back in and added, "Man, I can't believe Jo Beth made you this crazy."

Everything they say about redheads being spunky must be true. Most people know better than to harass a guy lifting weights.

Claire was only partly right about why I was acting so weird. Jo Beth calling it quits messed with my mind, but I wasn't really sure I was ever in love with her. I never experienced any dippy stuff like having a stereophonic Hootie & the Blowfish ballad ring in my ears when I saw her. I never wrote her a poem, carved her name into a scrub oak, or considered what we should name our kids. Still, after three years of dating she had become part of my life. I'd started to depend on Jo being there.

To tell you the truth, I was also mad that she was the one who got to do the dumping. Not that I was planning on ending things, but I always figured if it didn't work out between us, *I* would be the one to call it off.

I had just gone back to my arm curls and was thinking about ways I could make Jo Beth regret her decision (there had to be some way I could be photographed kissing Kathy Ireland) when the door opened and my friend Devin Schaub walked in. He looked real weird. Kind of spaced out.

"Yo, Dev! What's up? What are you doing here?"

"Oh, you know . . . . Tasha and I broke up today," he said matter-of-factly.

"No way, man! What happened?" Tasha had been Devin's girlfriend since homecoming—she's a total babe.

"Oh, you know." The dude seemed real out of it. He started wandering around my room as if he were in a gift shop, picking up things off the shelves and studying them.

"No, tell me. Did you break it off with her or vice versa?"

"Hard to say, really." He scratched his head. For some reason he wouldn't look me in the eye.

"Come on, Dev. What's the story?"

"Oh, you know."

"Why do you keep saying that? I *don't* know." I was getting kind of mad. Did he think I was some sort of expert on broken relationships?

Devin let out a long, miserable sigh and sat down on my bed. "I . . . I caught Tasha making out with Brad Culpepper in her living room," he said, staring down at the floor. "So I guess you could interpret it either way. She ditched me for someone better, or I ditched her for messing around."

"She was *what?* With *who?* Man, what a total two-faced bimbo! Culpepper too! So did you let him have it? Knock him around a few times?"

"Er, no. Not really."

"But you had it out with them, right?"

"Oh, yeah. Yeah. I told them off."

"Well, that's good. Dude'll probably be watching his back. Probably thinks you'll be running him down at every turn. What a jerk!"

"Yeah," he said, totally calm. He kept on looking around my room like he was planning to buy it. Poor guy seemed lost or something. I wasn't sure what he expected me to do or say. "Tough break, man" didn't seem to cover it.

"Culpepper's a snake," I told him. "Betcha anything Tasha will be running back to you all apologetic and stuff."

Dev didn't respond. I couldn't believe how cool

and calm he was. When Jo flaked out on me, the first thing I did was cowabunga that stupid horse. Then, before the game, I hightailed it home and whaled on the punching bag until my arms practically fell out of their sockets. But here Devin was, staring at my Jerry Rice poster, almost meditating.

We sat there silently for a few minutes. Devin kept studying the picture as if ol' Jerry was going to reach over, whack him on the shoulder, and say, "Yo, dude. Buck up." I was the one getting madder and madder.

The more I thought about it, the more unfair this whole girlfriend business seemed. Take me, for example. I was a great boyfriend. I always remembered birthdays and anniversaries, sent flowers, had the local DJ play her favorite song now and then, and for what? And Devin is a total upstanding dude. He's always holding doors open for girls and calling our female teachers "ma'am." He's the epitome of a sensitive guy, just like all the girls say they want. Well, all except Tasha Whitmeyer, I guess.

"This whole relationship thing is a crock!" I yelled out after a while. "I mean, what is it with women anyway? We do everything they want, and they still aren't happy. They're the ones that can't get it right. I'm telling you, Schaub. We'd be better off without them."

Devin barely nodded in reply, but I could tell I was getting to him. His cheeks were starting to spasm as he clenched and unclenched his jaw. I suddenly realized the whole reason he showed up was to get some answers from me, the way he usually did when it came to girls.

When I first met Devin in eighth grade, I wrote him off as a wimpy pretty boy. He just seemed too . . . wholesome. His dad coaches Little League, his mom plays the piano at our church, his younger brother, Damon, was state spelling bee champ for two years straight, and they all live in this tidy aqua blue house with a picket fence. I'm not kidding you—a *real* picket fence!

Anyway, we started getting to know each other in high school when we both went out for track. The dude can run! Our freshman coach was like this drill sergeant who kept barking out orders and calling us wusses if we cracked a sweat. All the other guys would whine and cry and threaten to quit, but not Devin. After a while he and I started hanging out. Now he's one of my best buddies.

Devin's tougher than he looks, and I've made it a personal mission these past couple of years to teach him how to act more cool. Unfortunately when it comes to girls, he's still kind of soft. Easy prey for broom-riding vixens like Tasha.

Women! I was beginning to see why some guys become priests or run off to join the merchant marines.

"Hey! I got it!" Somewhere in the boiling rage inside me I found a cool spot. A plan was starting to formulate. "I know a way to help you get over all this mess. You with me, man?"

"What?" he asked, hope flickering behind his baby blues. "What are you talking about?"

"Christmas break is coming up in a couple of weeks. What do you say we make it a *real* break? A break from girls."

Every Christmas my family goes skiing in Vail. It's totally rad. Standing on the side of a mountain and looking *down* on the clouds. Confetti-size snowflakes whirling about. Your face paralyzed by cold and velocity as you zigzag down the slope.

This year, unfortunately, it was the last place on earth I wanted to be. See, every Christmas, Jo Beth's family goes there too. And the thought of sitting around a ski resort with only one working leg and an ex-girlfriend lurking about seemed like one of those nightmares that turns your hair white. That's why my plan had to work.

I decided dinner would be the best time to suggest it. I sat patiently and made slow progress on the squash casserole. Sure enough, my dad eventually brought up the trip.

"This year I'm going to snowboard."

"*Dad!* Don't, please!" wailed Claire. "Remember last year? The ski basin officials asked you not to do the moguls anymore because too many people were tripping over your sprawled body."

"Well, this time I'm going to catch some radical drift, and if anyone doesn't like it, they can eat my powder."

My parents try to behave like teenagers—talking the talk, listening to our music, even going to the Horde festival with us. Plus they're always kissing each other in public like they're going steady instead of married. Sometimes it's cool to have hip parents. Other times (like when they attempted in-line skating) it's real embarrassing. Claire says they act that way to hold on to their "rapidly disappearing youth." She's such a know-it-all.

"I can see the news flash now." Claire shook her head. "'Oklahoma Dentist Causes Worst Avalanche in Colorado History.'"

"You know, Frank, maybe she's right. Maybe you should wait until next year, when Sean can teach you. I'd hate to have both of you hobbling around on crutches."

I sensed this was my big chance. "Um, Mom? I don't think I should go with you guys this vacation."

My folks exchanged surprised looks. "Why not?" my dad asked.

"Well, my knee is busted, and I'll just be sitting around anyway. Besides, I was thinking about Uncle Gary. I feel sorry for him spending Christmas alone ever since Grandma died. I thought I'd go visit him."

"So . . . you're doing this for Gary's sake?" my mom asked.

"Yeah, sure. Why not?"

"Come on. Get real!" Claire's voice was like a nail through my brain. "We all know the real reason you don't want to go. You're just avoiding—"

"And I thought we could give my nonrefundable plane ticket to one of Claire's friends," I cut in.

"Sounds good to me," Claire said, changing her tune faster than a heavy-metal DJ. "Lisa has always wanted to come with us."

"I'm sure Gary will have to work at the hotel most of the time. I hate to think of you sitting around alone on your Christmas break." Mom reached over and patted me on the arm.

"Got it covered, Mom. Devin says he'd go with me. He, um, needs to get away for a while. School's been stressing him out. And he's always wanted to see California."

"Oh? A couple of hunks cruising the California babes, huh?" My mom winked. You'd think she still subscribed to *Seventeen.*

"What do you say, guys? Can I go?"

My parents looked at each other for about two minutes without saying anything. I swear sometimes they're telepathic. Finally, when they broke their psychic connection, my dad said, "Well, I'm sorry you'll miss my big snowboarding debut. After supper you'd better call Gary and make sure he doesn't have plans."

Uncle Gary is totally cool. He lives out in California and works for a big hotel chain. He's got the perfect life: nice condo in Newport Beach. Sports car with a sunroof. And no wife or girlfriend around to tell him what to do. When I was ten, he taught me how to spit. He always gives the coolest gifts at Christmas, and he's the only relative who never told me to give up football and try to go into business. Sometimes when Mom and Dad had to go out of town for a few days, he'd fly over and stay with us. He'd let us stay up as late as we wanted, order lots of pizza, and even let me split a beer with him now and then. He was just the guy I needed to spend time with if I wanted to get over this girlfriend disaster.

I didn't recognize Uncle Gary's voice when he answered the phone. He sounded different, kind of low and breathy. I almost hung up.

"Hey, Uncle Scary? It's me, Sean. What's up, homey?"

"Oh! Sean! Hey, not much, buddy." His voice returned to its usual register. "I'm glad you called. I've got some big news for you. But first, tell me. Why are you calling me on a Saturday evening? You aren't in jail, are you?"

"No, nothing like that. But I do need a favor."

"Anything. Shoot."

"I was wondering if me and a friend could come hang with you during the Christmas break."

"No problem. I'd love it. We've got a lot to catch up on. So who's the 'friend'? You and Jo Beth aren't sneaking out here to elope, are you?"

"No way, man. Actually, that's part of the reason I'm coming." I lowered my voice and shut the door to my room. "Jo and I aren't together anymore. She ditched me, man. It was real ugly. And I was thinking I needed some real guy-bonding time. You know, no women allowed?"

"Er, yeah. Yeah. So, your mom's okay with this?"

"Totally cool. She, Dad, and Claire are probably eager to get rid of me. I've been kind of a jerk around here lately."

"I see." He paused for a few seconds. Then he cleared his voice and said, "Well, like I always say, my pad's your pad. And your friend's. You come on out, and we'll mend your manhood in no time. Heck, we'll make you bulletproof. How's that?"

"Thanks, Scary. I knew I could count on you. I'll call you later with the details. Oh, yeah. What's the big news you were going to share?"

"News? Oh, that. Yeah. Um . . . I got a promotion at work. Tell your mom before long all Hilton hotels will be renamed Gary's Place."

"Way to go!" I said. "Well, I better call the airlines and stuff. Thanks again, Uncle Gary, for . . . helping me out."

"Anytime."

After I hung up with Gary, I called Devin and told him the good news. He was totally stoked. But the hard part was still to come—convincing his folks to let him come along. They're the type of people who see holidays as high-powered family time. Big reunions. Lots of food. Aunt Bertha hugging you till your ribs crack. What kind of a break is that?

Devin said not to worry. He'd figure something out. His folks just *had* to let him come to California with me.

Two

Devin

I KNEW THERE was no way my folks would let me go to California with Sean.

My parents are the types who believe in strict curfews, homework completed before supper-time, skim milk, and thank-you cards. Their idea of a party involves punch, cookies, and a game of charades, and holidays followed a set of traditions handed down through generations. Needless to say, when I mentioned Sean's invitation to join him in California, I expected a lecture on the importance of family.

Was I ever shocked when my mom turned toward me, dabbed her eyes with a Kleenex, and said, "Well, you're eighteen years old. I guess you're becoming an adult now and should be able to make your own decisions."

So there I sat, returning my tray to the proper

upright position for landing while below us the colorful lights of Los Angeles twinkled brighter than the ones in the sky.

Sean folded his arms behind his head and nodded happily at the skyline. "Here we are," he announced, sighing contentedly. "Man, I feel like I just outjumped the safety for the winning six points."

"Yeah, the engines on this thing sound a lot like our marching band," I said dryly.

A long-legged flight attendant came down the aisle for one last check before landing.

"Take good notes," whispered Sean as she nodded at us approvingly. "She just might be the last female you'll see for a while." He sounded almost gleeful.

A few minutes later the plane made its noisy descent. At the same time I felt another sinking sensation in my gut. I couldn't shake the feeling that I might be making a mistake.

After I told Sean my folks would let me come, he'd done nothing but talk about that crazy no-girls-allowed plan of his. When I'd agreed to it at his house, I figured it was just a bunch of tough talk and that he'd let it drop after a while. But Sean was completely serious about the idea. He even kept referring to it as "our pact," as if it had been printed on paper and officially notarized.

I started to get the feeling that he and I had very different ideas about this trip. While I saw it as a chance to go somewhere, meet new people, and have fun, Sean envisioned it as a chance to get away from somewhere, avoid fifty percent of the local population, and repair his mangled ego. Still, I had to act like I was as fanatical about the pact as he was. Otherwise he would have thought I was the world's biggest sissy—and maybe I was.

You see, I kind of lied to Sean when I told him about yelling at Tasha. Truth is, when I walked in and saw them together, I just stood there like a dork. The music was so loud and they were so into what they were doing that they didn't even notice me right away. I don't know how long I stayed there frozen in shock with my mouth hanging open. Finally Tasha looked up and screamed.

Then Culpepper looked over and saw me.

"Oh, man. Schaub. Hey, dude, I'm sorry. We just . . . just . . ."

Just what? I thought. *She stole your last breath mint and you were trying to retrieve it? She wanted to test her long-lasting lip gloss on you?*

They stared at me stupidly, Tasha with her face all red and Brad with his Caesar haircut all messed up. I honestly wasn't angry at all. I was too disgusted to feel angry.

There didn't seem to be anything to say, so I just walked out and shut the door behind me. Later, after talking with Sean, I realized I should have reacted more strongly. Called them names or knocked over a couple of pieces of furniture. Anything except the wimpy way I just stood there and took it.

Maybe Sean's right, I thought. *Maybe two weeks without girls will make me feel like a man again.*

I figured I could learn something from Sean. Sean is one of those guys who is born cool—unlike me. He's always able to say things that make girls swoon. Me? I talk to women like I would anyone, polite and friendly. Sean says that's why I end up with more girls as friends instead of date prospects. He thinks I open up too much and act too chummy.

"You need to act more mysterious, dude," he's always telling me. "Girls like a challenge."

They must. Getting to know Sean is like climbing Mount Macho. He *never* opens up, and I've been one of his best friends for a couple of years now. But he's also the most loyal friend I've ever had. One word from me and Sean would have pounded Brad Culpepper into gravel, with no second thoughts. That's the type of buddy he is.

As the plane crept toward the terminal that same pretty flight attendant walked over and knelt down beside Sean.

"I noticed you had a knee brace. Maybe you'd like to deplane ahead of all the others to make sure you don't get hurt? I could help you if you like." Her voice was low and sexy.

Sean attracts women like charged electrons. Not only is he tall and broad shouldered, he's got one of those faces like a pinup guy. No kidding. He looks just like Leonardo DiCaprio, but with dark hair.

"Need some help standing up?" cooed the flight attendant.

Sean's back stiffened, as if he'd been challenged to a fight, and his eyes dropped to the floor. "No thanks," he said in a low voice. "We'll wait and get off last. I don't need any help."

"Okay," the woman said, sounding both surprised and offended. "Enjoy your stay in Los Angeles." She quickly walked away.

Guess Sean meant it when he said the "no girls allowed" mandate was in effect.

"He-e-ey, Sean!" someone yelled when we stepped out into the gate area. I assumed he was Sean's uncle. The man looked a lot like Sean except he was twenty years older and sported a goatee. "You're looking meaner and uglier every time I see you, boy. What's with the brace?"

"Long story. And who are you calling ugly? You can't hide behind that fur on your face, Uncle Scary."

Gary laughed heartily and hugged Sean, whacking his back like it was covered with bugs. Then he turned to me and gripped my hand so hard, I thought my fingers would fuse together.

"You must be Devin. Nice to meet you," he said.

"Same here. Thanks for letting us stay with you, sir."

"The queen hasn't knighted me yet. You can call me Gary. Or Uncle Scary, like baby Claire used to. How is my Claire Bear anyway?" He turned back toward Sean, and the three of us made our way to the baggage-claim area.

"Spoiled rotten. She sends her best. My folks too. I'll tell you all about them, but then no more talk about women. *Any* women. Including Mom or Claire. If this thing's going to work, we can't make any exceptions."

"Got it," Gary said. "From now on I won't mention . . . uh . . . the soft, lumpy gender."

We walked forever through the bustling airport and finally ended up at the baggage area. As we stood in front of the carousel with our flight number above it, a weird-looking guy walked up and stood next to us.

Sean and I had seen our share of radicals. Our high school has a couple of skaters who wear baggy pants and shaggy hairdos. Vonda Gilstrap, our resident social protester, once dyed her hair green for Earth Day. And one of those gamer fanatics wears black every day and tells people to call him Mordred.

This guy, though, was real scary. I mean pull-out-your-crosses-and-pray unearthly looking. Even Sean, who I happen to know isn't scared of anyone, looked kind of uncomfortable. The guy had a long jet black ponytail that was more grease than hair, dark eye makeup, tattoos up and down his bare arms, and metal drilled into every exposed section of his body: ears, nose, mouth, eyebrows, cheeks. It was painful just looking at him. Then, when he leaned forward to hoist up a black leather satchel, his vest fell open and I could see large hoops stabbed through each nipple. I didn't know whether I should spray him with Mace or Bactine! No telling how he got past the metal detector.

"I take it small-town Oklahoma hasn't caught on to these fashions yet?" Gary whispered, nodding toward our acupuncture specimen.

"Not exactly," I said.

"Well, welcome to California, home to the stars and other space cases."

After Sean and I retrieved our suitcases, we followed Gary out to the parking garage.

"Hey, what happened to your Corvette?" Sean asked when Gary unlocked the rear hatch of a shiny gold Landcruiser.

"Sold it," Gary explained. "I got tired of having no room for passengers or stuff. Plus sports cars are the vehicle of choice for rich teenagers and men in a middle-age crisis. I figured I'll never be mistaken for the former, and I didn't want to be stereotyped as the latter."

I didn't say much on the drive to Gary's house. While he and Sean relived old times, I stared out the window at the passing scenery. I couldn't see much since it was so dark, but I did make out some palm trees and could see the faint line of the ocean in the distance. It looked beautiful—postcard California. But whenever I saw a neon Santa Claus or a lighted Christmas tree in someone's window, I felt a slight pang for home.

Eventually we arrived at a beachfront condo

called The Palo Duro, a tall white building with a Mediterranean-looking courtyard out front. Real swanky. We could hear the ocean and the seagulls and smell the salt in the breeze.

Just as I was starting to feel excited Gary unlocked his door and led us inside. Immediately my gut seized up. I don't know what I expected. Maybe a fake tiger-skin bedspread on a giant water bed, a framed poster of a Ferrari Testarossa, or some strategically placed mirrors—your typical, Hugh Hefner-style bachelor pad. This scene was very different.

There was a kitchen with two bar stools along the counter, a small dinette set covered with office files, a leather couch, a ratty-looking recliner, a coffee table, and a TV. Nothing else. I mean *nothing.* My dad's camper was homier than this. There weren't even any pictures on the wall. And no Christmas decorations whatsoever.

"You fellows make yourselves comfortable and I'll go get Sean's other bag," Gary said as he stepped back outside.

Comfortable? I wondered. *In this place?*

"Man, I'm parched," Sean announced, settling onto the couch. "You want something to drink, Dev?"

"Yeah. I'll get it."

As I went through the cupboards looking for glasses I noticed dozens of canned food items. Ravioli, tuna, cocktail weenies. The only things in the fridge were soda and beer. No real food at all. I imagined us sitting along the bar on Christmas Day, eating canned chili and macaroni and cheese with some Twinkies for dessert. Suddenly I longed for home even more. *Why did I ever agree to this?*

"Thanks," Sean said as I handed him his Coke. "Isn't this great? Just like I told you."

"Yeah," I answered, trying to match his enthusiasm. "It's cool."

Just then Gary came back in, carrying the suitcase and a couple of quilts.

"Here we go," he said, setting the blankets on the couch. "I had to borrow these from Alex, my neighbor across the hall. I'm a little short on linens. One of you can take the bed in the office; the other will have to sleep out here on the couch. I'd let you have my room, but I just sleep on the floor."

What was this guy? A monk?

"That's okay," Sean said. "We don't care where we sleep, do we, Dev?"

"No. Not at all."

"Great. Hey, you guys hungry? I could warm up some ravio—"

"No. Thank you," I interrupted. "If you don't mind, I think I'll just turn in. I'm real tired all of a sudden."

"No way, dude! It's our first day of vacation. Let's hang out and watch *Saturday Night Live* or something."

"I would, but my head hurts and I thought I'd . . . rest up for all the stuff we want to do."

My explanation seemed to appease Sean, and we agreed that he'd take the couch so he could watch some late night TV and I'd crash in Gary's office.

The "office" was a tiny room down the hall that was furnished in the same minimalistic style as the rest of the place. It had a NordicTrack, a shelf crammed full of Tom Clancy novels, and a futon. The latter was already pulled flat and covered with two tissue-thin sheets and a wool blanket.

The man is in his thirties and he lives like a college student, I thought glumly. *If this is a guys-only lifestyle, count me out.*

The next day I got up early and decided to go for a run. I had made up my mind to stop feeling sorry for myself and thought a jog along the beach would help me clear my head.

Sean was snoring on the coach. A half-eaten can of ravioli sat on the coffee table, and a sports magazine lay open on his chest. I had already heard Gary get up and leave for his long drive to Los Angeles, where he worked.

As quietly as I could, I put on my running clothes and slipped out the door. I was glad I'd packed a good jacket. Even though it wasn't cold, there was a slight breeze and a drizzly mist filled the air.

I jogged along the sidewalk that runs parallel to the beach and took in the sights. It was nice and peaceful. Very few people were out, and the waves crashing against the shore added an extra rhythm to my footfall. On the other side of the sidewalk—to my right—stood rows and rows of tall, narrow condos, crammed together like matches. Then came a row of pastel-colored beach houses, each with a huge porch adorned with couches, hammocks, swings, and wind chimes made of shells.

After a while I came upon a shop-lined stretch of beach opposite a long wooden pier. I stopped and stretched my legs, then decided to get something to drink. Most of the stores weren't open yet, so I strolled along, looking at the merchandise in the display windows—beachwear, surfboards, souvenirs, cigars, arts-and-crafts items. I passed a couple of eclectic-looking cafés, but they looked closed too. Finally I found a coffee shop with its lights on. The sign above the door said Blinkers—Serving Planet Earth Since 1985.

The only person inside was a guy behind the counter. He was wearing a 49ers cap and jacket, and his back was to me as he refilled some containers of sugar.

"Um, excuse me," I said, but got no response. "Sir? Excuse me, sir?" Still no response. I cleared my throat and said, "Pardon me? Are you open?" He continued to ignore me.

"Hello-o?" I sang out, starting to get perturbed.

Finally the guy saw my reflection in the mirror across from him, let out a little yelp of surprise, and swung around to face me.

But instead of a surfer dude's blank stare two

beautiful—and very feminine—green eyes met my gaze. "Oh, I'm sorry!" she exclaimed, yanking a pair of headphones off her ears. "I didn't expect anyone this early, especially on a Sunday. I just got here a little while ago and haven't even finished setting up."

The girl wriggled out of her jacket and took the hat off her head, releasing a cascade of chestnut brown locks. Then she disappeared behind the counter and started fiddling with some switches. Soft jazz music suddenly drifted out.

"Welcome to Blinkers," she said, popping back up again. "Can I help you?"

I must have had the most idiotic stare on my face. For a second I forgot why I'd come in.

"Boy, are you in need of caffeine." She grinned. "Can I get you some coffee?"

I just stood there, mesmerized. She was so pretty: green eyes flashing under winglike lashes, glossy brown hair, ivory skin. Plus she had this incredible smile that pushed her cheeks up into soft, rosy balls and pointed her delicate chin, making her face look like a giant valentine.

Eventually I found my voice. "You got any orange juice?"

"Yew gawt any arnge juice," she repeated back to me, reaching into a refrigerated case for a plastic juice bottle. "Where are you from anyway?"

I paused for a second, trying to figure out if she was making fun of me. I couldn't tell. "Oklahoma," I said finally.

"Oh. What brings you to Newport Beach?"

"My buddy and I are visiting his uncle for Christmas break."

"Ah, a high-school boy," she remarked, nodding at my Saddle Pass Pirates jacket. "You a senior?"

"Uh, yeah."

"So am I. Although I'm not getting much of a break." She gestured toward the cash register and espresso machine.

"I see. So what do other people do for fun around here?"

"You picked the wrong season for fun. This is a beach."

"I noticed."

"And unfortunately," she continued, "the weather has been lousy lately."

"Hmmm. Any movie stars live around here?"

She snorted. "Are you kidding? Not even their drug dealers live here."

I sighed and stared out the window at the rough ocean water. "There's got to be a perfect moment here somewhere," I mumbled absently.

"What did you say? A what?"

"Perfect moment."

"What is that? Some New Age philosophy?"

"No, it's from that movie *Swimming to Cambodia*. You seen it?" Her furrowed brow told me she hadn't, so I went on. "Every vacation has a perfect moment. Even if the trip is pretty lousy, there's usually one big moment that stands out." She gave me a blank stare.

"For example," I continued, "when my family and I camped at Yellowstone, it was seeing a mama bear and her two cubs strolling by the lake just as the sun was coming up. During our Six Flags trip it was when my cousin wet his pants on the Cliffhanger ride."

"Aha . . . I see. And you're wondering where your perfect moment is in this place."

"Or maybe this will be the first vacation without one." I took a swig of my orange juice.

"You seem a little too angst-ridden for this hour of the morning. Are you sure you don't want any caffeine?"

"No thanks. I have to jog all the way back. Caffeine messes up my heart rate."

"Aha," she said again. I felt like a lab specimen she was sizing up. "I should've known you were a runner. Where have you been jogging?"

"Just along the sidewalk. I think I cleaned off all the gum wads with my shoes."

"You should run along the beach instead. It's a much better workout," she said authoritatively.

"Says who?"

"Says me. That's how I got here. Nothing but sand on the bottoms of my shoes."

"Doesn't it hurt your ankles?"

"Not if you do it right and stretch out before and after. Hmmm . . . tell you what." She studied me again with intense scrutiny, cocking her head and tapping her chin with her index finger. "We could meet tomorrow morning and run together. What do you say?"

"Sure," I said, trying not to sound too eager.

"I'll play tour guide and tell you all the local gossip, maybe help you decide where your perfect moment can be found."

"Sounds great. Where should we meet?"

"I could take the bus in and meet you anyplace. Where are you staying?"

I paused for a minute, wondering what to do. Sean would bust my butt if he knew I was meeting a girl. "Uh . . . how 'bout we meet on the beach in front of the Palo Duro condo? I'd ask you to come up, but my roommate sleeps real late, you know?"

"I understand. Is seven o'clock too early? I have to be here in time to open at eight."

"No problem. See you at seven," I said, then started to walk out.

"Wait!" she called. I stopped in place and glanced back at her. "I don't know your name," she said.

"It's Devin. What's yours?"

"Halle."

"Halle," I repeated. I stared back at her for a moment, then exited the coffee shop in a daze.

It wasn't until I neared the condo courtyard that I realized I'd never paid her for the orange juice.

Three

Sean

OUR FIRST MORNING at Uncle Gary's, I woke up late. Gary had already gone to work but had left some cash on the kitchen counter next to a note that said, *Stock up—get whatever you need. See you later.* And Devin had left me a note saying he went out for a run. I was hungry and feeling jazzed about our first real day of female-free living, so I decided to cook my famous Sean Burgers for lunch.

I grabbed the money from the counter and went to the grocery store across the street to get what I needed. It took me forever—there was lots of weird stuff there that I'd never seen before. Next to the deli counter they had this gigantic refrigerated case full of fish, even stuff like shark and crab and something with purple tentacles.

Then when I got to the meat counter, I felt like a complete dork. I asked the dude there if they had hamburger patties, and he asked, "What kind?"

Not sure what he meant, I replied, "The round kind."

He looked at me as if I were still in diapers and said, "I meant what kind of burgers are you going to make? Tofu? Tempeh? Macrobiotic? Soy? Ostrich meat? Emu? Turkey?"

"Uh . . . don't you have any regular meat? Like from a cow?"

He nodded impatiently, causing his dreadlocks to bob up and down. "Would you like lean, superlean, hormone-free lean, or nonirradiated hormone-free lean?"

During our *Grapes of Wrath* unit in English last year we'd talked about how California was known as the land of plenty. But this was ridiculous.

After buying some meat I limped around the store and loaded up on other essentials: ketchup, mustard, Worcestershire sauce, buns, pickles, potato chips, Cheez Whiz, frozen egg rolls, root beer, and Pop-Tarts for breakfast.

I was feeling stoked about our stay. No girls for two whole weeks! It had only been a few hours, and already I felt more relaxed. Maybe bachelor life was the way to go. Gary never settled down, and he was totally happy. In fact, he was probably one of the most together dudes I'd ever known. My folks have it pretty good, and so do

Devin's, but they're like the exception to the rule. Most of my other friends' parents are divorced. Maybe this whole relationship business was just a bogus hard sell that society puts on us, when staying single was the key to real happiness.

And the more I thought about it, the more I realized that I could never really understand girls. Jo Beth was always trying to analyze me and talk about all sorts of serious stuff. Personal things like my hopes, dreams, worries, medical history, and animal I identify with the most. It's not that I don't think about stuff like that—I do. But who wants to talk about all that on a date? I mean, she was supposed to be my girlfriend, not my psychiatrist.

When I got back to the condo, I put all the groceries away except for the Sean Burger ingredients and got ready to create my masterpiece. It's the only thing I know how to cook. Gary and I created the recipe when he was staying with us a couple of years ago. The secret is to pour Worcestershire sauce on the patties while they're frying so that the flavor gets all soaked in.

I was all set to fire up the skillet and start cooking when I realized Gary didn't have a spatula. I checked all the cabinets, drawers, and dishwasher shelves but only found a couple of knives and a bottle opener. I figured Gary probably ate out all the time, so he didn't do much cooking at home. (More evidence of how fulfilling single life could be.) But there was no way I could make the burgers without a spatula.

I remembered Gary's mention of his neighbor Alex, the one who lent us the blankets. Maybe he'd have a spatula.

I walked across the hall and knocked on the front door. Alex was probably another California condo bachelor, so he might not have much except knives and forks either. But it was worth a try.

I was totally unprepared for what happened next.

The door opened, and I found myself face-to-face with the most incredible-looking girl I'd ever seen in my life. She had this exotic look about her, like an Egyptian princess or something. Dark, catlike eyes, high cheekbones, and a long, straight nose that punctuated her perfect features like an exclamation point. Her long black hair was so thick and shiny, I probably could've checked my reflection in it—which, considering I hadn't run a comb through my own hair since the day before, I suddenly had an urge to do.

"Yes? Can I help you?" she asked.

One look at her and I went into total brain lock. I couldn't even remember what state I was in. I stood there stupidly staring into her Cleopatra eyes and swallowing like I'd just crawled in from the high desert.

I must be at the wrong door, I thought, glancing around.

"Yes?" she asked again, starting to seem a little nervous. "Can I help you?"

"Oh, uh, yeah." I blinked hard and shook my

head a little, trying to restart some mental activity. "Can I borrow a spatula?"

Her wide, worried eyes narrowed into a look of confusion. "Who wants it?" she asked.

"I do."

"And you are . . . ?"

"Oh. Sorry. I'm Sean Foster. Gary McGonagle's nephew."

"Oh, yeah!" she exclaimed, warmth overcoming her face as she relaxed. "Gary's mentioned you. You're a senior, right? Just like me. My name's Alexandra—Alexandra Lopez. But you can call me Alex. Come on in."

She stepped aside and I hobbled through the doorway, forcing myself to take my eyes off her. *She's just a girl, Foster,* I told myself. *Don't wig out or anything.*

"Please excuse the mess. We're busy decorating the place for Christmas, but *someone* isn't helping me out much."

The living room was full of open cardboard boxes, each containing a glittering assortment of tinsel and glass ornaments. Sitting in the middle of the decorations was the "someone" she had loudly referred to. A little boy, probably about eight years old, sat in front of the television with a sour look on his face.

"This is my brother, Gabriel. Gabriel, this is Sean."

"Hey," he mumbled without taking his eyes off the TV set.

"If you don't mind waiting a second, I'll see if I

can find our spatula. It might take a while. I've been baking, and the kitchen is a total wreck." She turned and with a ripple of her glossy hair disappeared from sight, making me wonder if she was one of those angelic visions all the tabloids talk about.

I sat on the couch and turned my attention to the football game on the TV. "Who's playing?" I asked.

The kid turned slowly toward me, and judging by the look on his face, I half expected him to say, "Why should I tell you?" Instead he scrunched his eyes up at me and replied, "Dallas and New York."

"Ah. Who's winning?"

"The Giants are up by seven."

"Who are you rooting for?"

He shrugged absentmindedly, so I figured he probably wasn't into discussing things. Instead we watched Troy Aikman launch a long pass toward the end zone.

"Aw, man! That call was totally bogus!" I yelled, leaping off the couch and shaking my fist at the ref on TV.

The boy looked up at me as if I were some sort of deranged terrorist that had broken into his living room. "What did they do wrong?" he asked.

"The ref said that Irvin was out of bounds in the end zone, but he had both feet down. Watch the replay. His toes touch down in the end zone. His momentum makes him skid out of bounds without taking another step, but that doesn't matter since he already made contact in bounds.

Technically it should be a touchdown."

Right after I explained all this, a commentator's voice came on saying pretty much the same thing. The kid looked from me to the TV and back again, his eyes widening.

"Wow. How do you know so much about football?"

"I play it."

"You do? Are you a quarterback?"

"No, I'm a wide receiver. Like Michael Irvin, only better."

"Really? Is that how you got hurt?" he asked, glancing at my leg.

"Yep," I replied. I gave him a brief account of how I got injured, reenacting the play as much as my knee brace and the living-room furniture would allow. As I talked I could see him loosen up and drop the attitude. His eyes got bigger, his mouth dropped open, and he kept saying "wow" or "whoa" over and over again. It was cool having someone gush about my football adventures. So I went on a bit about some of the stellar plays I'd made and body-crushing tackles I'd been in.

"Dontcha get scared, like when all those other guys come running after you?"

"Nah. I used to, but if you let them rattle you, you'll play real lame. I just train hard and stay focused. Besides, I have a lucky charm that protects me."

"You do?" he asked, his eyes bulging.

"Yep. Take a look at this." I reached into my wallet and took out my autographed Jerry Rice player card. "See? My uncle Gary gave me this when I first started on varsity. Since then I've never messed up—well, almost never."

"Whoa. Cool!" he exclaimed, running his index finger over the photo.

"Hey, you look like you could be a football player someday. You look solid enough. And I bet you're fast, huh?"

"I sure am," he said, puffing up with pride. "I even beat my daddy in a race once, didn't I, Alex?"

I whirled around to see Alex standing behind me with a spatula in her hand. I wondered how long she'd been standing there.

"Yes, Gabriel, you did," Alex answered with a funny expression on her face. Then she gave me a different kind of strange look. Her mouth was half smiling, but her eyes were scrunched up in a questioning stare. It reminded me of the way my mom looks at my dad whenever they have that weird mind-link thing between them. Unfortunately the only thing I could pick up was my own heartbeat, thumping like a subwoofer.

"Hey, Alex. Did you know this guy's a football player? He's going to be famous."

"Don't call him 'this guy,' Gabriel. It isn't polite. His name's Sean."

"Sean is going to be just like Michael Irvin. Only better."

"That's great," she said, looking at me like I was doing a magic trick or something. Then she turned back to her brother. "Gabriel, say good-bye to Sean now. You have to go downstairs and wait for Grandma. She's taking you to the mall for some new shoes, remember?"

"Aw, man. Do I hafta go? She thinks I'm a baby. She won't let me go in the arcade or nothing."

"Go downstairs *now.* Before I throw you out the window."

"Okay, okay," he grumbled. "Bye, Sean. Maybe you could come see my football card collection sometime? Will ya?"

"Sure. Sounds cool. You go get some rad shoes now. Remember, they're the most important piece of equipment we athletes own."

He smiled up at me and then ran to the front door. "See?" he said excitedly. "I really am fast." Then he disappeared out into the hallway. We could hear the pounding of his feet as he raced all the way down the corridor toward the stairwell.

Alex smiled. "You're good with kids, aren't you? Do you have younger brothers and sisters?"

"I have a little sister, Claire, but I'm no good with her. We fight all the time."

"So do Gabriel and I. Especially lately." She paused for a second and took a deep breath. "You see, our dad died in a boating accident back in February."

"Oh. I'm . . . I'm sorry." I felt horrible for her, but I had no idea what to say.

"Thanks." Alex met my eyes briefly, then stared down at the floor. "It's been a tough year. My mom's a nurse, and she has to work lots of extra shifts now so we don't lose the condo. That means I'm always having to watch Gabriel when we're not in school. It isn't easy. He really resents me telling him what to do, and he's been so sullen and withdrawn."

"I'm sorry," I said again.

"You've really seemed to reach him, though. He seems to like you."

"He's a great kid. I do like him."

She stared at me with that same penetrating look she flashed me earlier—kind of sad and grateful and amazed all at the same time.

I had a sudden urge to reach over and touch her. She seemed so fragile. I know it sounds totally bizarre, but I just wanted to hold her and tell her everything would be okay.

Suddenly I realized what was happening. I was starting to let a girl mess with my emotions. I felt bad for Alex and her family, but I couldn't let her beautiful eyes and somber looks distract me from my no-girls pact with Devin. I had to get out of there before I fell under her spell even more.

"Um, I need to get back to Gary's. I'm supposed to be making lunch, and it's getting kind of late."

"No problem. I understand. Here, don't forget this," she said, handing me the spatula. Then she gave me a huge smile that made my insides go all spongy again.

"Well . . . see ya!" I called out before quickly opening the door and stepping into the hallway.

"Bye, Sean. It was nice meeting you," she said.

I stood in the hallway for a second after she closed the door and took a deep breath. When I turned around, I noticed a woman in front of Gary's door, writing something on a Post-it pad. She looked like she was in her thirties and was a total babe.

Jeez, I'm surrounded in this place, I thought. *How can I avoid women when they keep showing up everywhere?*

I froze in my tracks and watched her, wondering what was going on. Eventually she tore off the note, pressed it against the door so that it stuck, and started to walk off. As she passed me she gave me a big smile and said, "Good afternoon."

Could she be selling something? I wondered. I thought about asking her if she was looking for Gary, but she was already stepping onto the elevator. I took down the note and read it as I walked back into the condo. It said: *Came by, but no one was home. I'll try again later—Julie.*

Weird. No last name or anything. Just "Julie." I wondered if she could be a business associate of Gary's.

At that moment Devin came in, tracking sand all over the place.

"Hey," he said.

"Hey. How was your jog?"

"Great!" he responded with a big smile. "I think I'm going to really like it here. It's really . . . beautiful."

"See?" I said. "This trip has already been good

for you. I hope you're hungry—I'm making my famous Sean Burgers." I waved the spatula at him.

The phone rang. I set down the spatula and picked up the receiver. It was Gary.

"Hey, Sean. How's it going? You guys finding everything okay? Did you go get some food? I know the place is a bit barren."

"Yeah, thanks for leaving the cash, Gary. We're great. Dev just got back from a jog, and he already looks like a new man. All play and no women seems to be paying off for us."

"Glad to hear it."

"Oh. Speaking of, some woman named Julie came by for you."

"Really? Oh, um, what did she say?"

"Nothing. I was out, er, getting stuff for lunch, but she left a note on the door." I read him the message, then asked, "So, who is she?"

"Her? Nobody. She's just . . . someone I hired to come by and clean the place a couple of times a week."

"Oh. Well, come home soon, man. I'm making Sean Burgers and the San Francisco game is on in an hour."

"Okay, I'll be there in a little while. And if you need anything, my neighbor Alex across the hall can help you out. She's a real sweetheart."

She certainly is, I thought, remembering her dazzling smile and stellar eyes.

"Thanks, Gary, but I don't need her help. I'll do just fine without her."

Four

Devin

OUR SECOND MORNING in California, I woke up early again and got ready to meet Halle for our jog. The night before, Sean and I had stayed up late watching some dumb horror movie and eating salty potato chips until my mouth felt raw. I finally got to bed around 2 A.M., and my watch alarm went off at six-thirty. But thinking about Halle was all it took to jettison me from the futon.

For an entire day I grappled with my conscience over whether I should tell Sean about my date with Halle. I eventually decided I shouldn't since Sean was so into his no-girls-allowed campaign. Plus the logical section of my brain pointed out that jogging with Halle wasn't technically a date. Then my epidermal layer urged me to keep mum too since it had no desire to take a pummeling from Sean's bare knuckles.

But the more I thought about it, the more senseless this whole guys-only pact seemed. Sean was just mad at the world after Jo Beth dumped him. I could tell the breakup really messed with his mind, and he probably wanted to punish all females by denying them his dimpled smile. I, on the other hand, didn't really see this as a "break" from girls, mainly because I didn't have the luck with them that Sean did. How can you take a break from something you rarely have?

Tasha and I only went out for a couple of months. She'd just moved from Missouri, and since all the other kids in Saddle Pass have known each other since kindergarten, she was automatically shrouded in intrigue—the beautiful woman with the mysterious past. So when she agreed to go out with me, I thought I'd hit the major leagues as far as date worthiness was concerned.

Sean was almost as pleased about the whole thing as I was. He saw it as my opportunity to act more cool with a girl. I wouldn't listen to him, though. I figured the fact that she was interested meant she liked me for who I really was. Unfortunately after two months of the real me, she went looking for someone else. But after getting to know *her* better, I found I didn't like her much anyway. She was kind of spoiled and self-centered. Still, the Tasha experience was enough to make me take Sean's advice more seriously.

I quickly threw on my running suit, brushed

my hair and teeth as quietly as I could, and tiptoed out through the living room. Sean lay sprawled on the couch like an accident victim. One hand grasped the back cushion as if he was trying to hold on for dear life; the other arm lay across his eyes. His injured leg was propped on the coffee table and the other was contorted at a strange angle. I decided I shouldn't be too bummed about the lumpy futon.

Halle was already on the beach doing stretches when I got there. She had on her 49ers jacket, her hair was up in a sleek ponytail, and an incredible length of slender, curvy legs separated her white Nikes and black wind shorts.

"Hi!" she called out. "I wasn't sure you were going to show up."

"Why? I'm not late, am I?"

"No, but we sort of made hasty plans. Plus you owe me a dollar and fifteen cents. I thought maybe you were some slick con man who gets out of paying for drinks by distracting female cashiers with those blue eyes of yours."

I blushed, partly from her compliment and partly because she had just turned and bent down to stretch her calves, causing her shorts to rise dangerously high.

"Well, uh, actually *I* was the one that got distracted and forgot to pay. Sorry about that. I brought the money today."

"No problem." She stood back up. "It's on me. A welcome-to-California drink. So, are you ready?"

I had been so busy talking and staring at her legs that I hadn't done any stretches yet.

"Oh, uh, almost. I should warm up a bit more."

"Okay," she said. "But we do need to get going soon if I'm gonna make it in time to open the coffee shop."

I bent over to touch my hands to the ground and loosen my back leg muscles, but she bent over at the same time. *Bam!* Our foreheads collided like a couple of billiard balls, sending us each sprawling backward onto the sand.

"Ouch!" she cried, throwing her hands up to her head.

"I'm so sorry! Are you okay?"

Halle slowly lifted her face and looked at me. Her brow was scrunched up—no doubt in the same throbbing pain that was drumming inside me—but her mouth curled into a smile.

Then she burst out laughing. "Oh! Ow! It hurts to laugh," she said, giggling even more.

I started to laugh too, all the while marveling at her sense of humor. Halle's laughter was irresistible—a shriek of delight followed by a short musical scale.

I helped her stand up, and we took a minute to collect ourselves and brush the sand off our clothes.

"You ready now?" she asked after a moment.

I decided to forgo any further stretching and just run cold. "Sure."

"Okay. Now, running on the beach is a bit

different from running on a sidewalk or track. Unlike concrete, sand gives under your weight. But unlike a track, it doesn't spring back any. So you need to push off a bit more with your foot. It takes some getting used to."

We began to run and, as she had warned, it took me some time to find a good stride. Luckily, though, I didn't stumble and knock her into the surf or anything.

Along the way Halle showed me a few interesting local spots. "See that tall brown building over there?" She pointed toward the nearby street. "It used to be the headquarters for a big smuggling ring."

"What did they smuggle?"

"You name it. And see that restaurant down the road? Elvis snuck in there all the time to order BLTs."

"Really?"

"Yup. Oh! You'll love this next one—see this yellow beach house coming up? The lady who lives there actually collects toilets."

"No way!"

"I'm not kidding. She has tons of them. They did a story about her on *Hard Copy* and everything."

"I bet her guests feel funny when she offers them a seat."

Halle laughed that songbird laugh of hers and elbowed me. "Welcome to the real Newport Beach. We might not have the plastic and glitz of

Disneyland, the diamonds of Beverly Hills, or the . . . silicone of Hollywood, but we have our share of drama and intrigue. You'll find your perfect moment someplace around here."

"I'm sure I will," I said, staring over at her. It was tough managing to stay on my feet while we ran. Not because of the sand but because I often found myself watching Halle instead of where I was going.

"Tell me about your hometown," she said, smiling. "Is it as terribly exciting as this place?"

"Saddle Pass? There's not much to tell. Small town about a half hour outside of Tulsa. Five traffic lights, two strip malls, and a nearby creek. The only real entertainment is high-school football games. Otherwise we drive to Tulsa."

"Jeez, you make it sound pretty backwoods. You guys wear shoes, right?"

I smiled and shook my head, enjoying the feel of the ocean air as we ran. "It's small, but not as behind the times as you'd think. Anyway, progress is about to hit. Next spring they're opening a Wal-Mart!" I opened my arms in a grand gesture.

"Oh, joy!" she exclaimed, wrinkling up her nose. "Is that really the height of culture there? Do you ever feel like you're missing out on stuff?"

"Nah, not really. I mean, we don't have a fancy opera house or anything, but we have what matters. Everyone knows everyone. There isn't much crime. It sounds silly to say so, but we have good old-fashioned values in Saddle Pass." I shut my mouth immediately and looked down at my feet hitting the sand. *Ugh! That sounded corny even to me! Sean's right. Know when to can it, Dev.*

"Sounds like it's done all right by you," Halle said, feigning a southern drawl. "What do you say we stop and walk the rest of the way? We're almost there."

I was grateful for her suggestion. Not enough sleep and too little stretching were starting to take their toll, and all that talking had left me out of breath. I needed to shut up—for lots of reasons.

Sean's strategy to avoid all women was a good idea for him, maybe. I, on the other hand, now had a chance to reinvent myself. With Halle, I could start over from scratch and be the type of guy girls seem to want—a guy like Sean. And cool guys don't blab their life stories when they first meet someone.

Halle and I stopped jogging and sat down on the sand to stretch.

"Are you okay?" she asked. "You look kind of worn out. I told you the beach was a tougher run."

"Yeah, well, I just had a rough night. That's all."

"Oh? Hot date?" She raised an eyebrow.

I was about to say, "Are you kidding?" but then remembered Sean's advice: Be mysterious. "I watched a lame horror movie," I said, shrugging. "The scariest part about it was that it wouldn't end." There, that was sort of ambiguous. At least she didn't know who I saw the movie with.

"Your eyes do look bloodshot. But they go well with that red welt on your forehead where we crashed into each other. Here, let me take a look."

She leaned in toward me to inspect my wound. I could feel her warm breath on my cheek and smell the flowery scent of her hair.

"Ooh—I think you're going to have a little bump here." She brushed her fingers lightly over my forehead. Suddenly whatever pain I felt melted away. Instead a searing heat traveled down from the top of my head. I half expected my hair to burst into flames.

She took her hand away, and I reached up and touched her forehead. "I . . . um." I was about to apologize again for slamming into her, but I made myself stop. "I feel something too," I said softly.

For a few seconds we just sat there staring at each other, my fingers lightly stroking her brow. Her wide eyes darted from one of my eyes to the other, as if searching for something. And it might have been an optical illusion, but it seemed every breath she took brought her a tiny bit closer to me.

All of a sudden I felt self-conscious. I had a weird notion that she could look right into me, past all the pretense, seeing me as the shy, awkward loser I really was. Plus there were people walking nearby. It probably looked like I was attempting the Vulcan mind probe on her or trying to do some faith healing. I quickly averted my eyes and brought my hand down.

"Uh, maybe I'll get some coffee today," I

mumbled. "I could use the caffeine. Besides, I think I've already hit my target heart rate." *And beyond!*

We strolled silently the rest of the way to the coffee shop. As we walked I felt totally clueless. Should I have tried to kiss her back there on the beach? Or said something suave and romantic? She didn't exactly seem repulsed by me, but then again, we barely knew each other.

When we arrived at the coffee shop, Halle unlocked the front door and turned on the lights.

"Are you the only one working here this morning?" I asked, trying to break the weird silence between us.

"No. Bowman's coming in, but he's in a band and the earliest we can get him here is nine."

"Oh? Who's Bowman?" A little tinge of insecurity started to gnaw at my gut.

"This high-school dropout whose only abilities are playing bass and making a mean cup of espresso. He's harmless—not exactly a deep thinker or anything—but he's sweet. My dad hired him because he looks so bohemian. The customers love that."

"Your father owns the place?"

"Yep. He bought it when I was five."

"Does your mom work here too?"

"No. She's . . . um . . . not around anymore." Halle's normally sunny face suddenly grew stormy. "About the same time Dad bought this place, my mom took off with his former business partner."

"Uh. Gee, I'm sorry," I stammered, sounding even more like Beaver Cleaver. I felt horrible for having brought up the subject. "We don't have to talk about this if you don't want to."

"It's okay," she said, shrugging resignedly. "I figure the sordid tale will come out eventually."

Even though the moment was awkward, I liked the way she said that—eventually—as if she knew we'd be seeing more of each other.

Halle took a deep breath and looked down at the counter. "See, my dad and this guy used to run a restaurant together, only, well, things got . . . complicated. Mom ran off with the jerk and married him. She's still with him too."

"Do you see her much?"

"Nah. They live in Boston now and have two little boys of their own. I only seem to get called for a visit when they need free baby-sitting."

She twisted her face into a scowl and started noisily lining up sugar canisters along the counter.

"Here, let me fill those for you," I said, taking a huge bag of sugar from her hands.

"Thanks." She smiled and took a deep breath, seeming to snap back into the present. "So, what about your parents? Any soap operas at your house?"

"Oh, they're just your average mom and dad. My father's an assistant principal at the local elementary school, and Mom teaches piano to the neighborhood kids. I have a little brother, Damon, who's twelve. We're pretty close, I guess." Once again I was painfully aware of how sugary sweet my life seemed—especially compared to her family. How could I seem cool and mysterious when I lived a Brady Bunch existence?

"Sounds nice."

"It's all right. Nothing special."

Halle cocked her head and pondered me. "I bet your future is just as rosy as your past. What are your plans for after high school?"

"I don't know. Probably major in communications somewhere. I'm looking at a few different schools right now. What about you?"

"I want to get a business degree and specialize in restaurant management," she said, gesturing to the walls around her. "After helping out in this place for practically my whole life, I have lots of ideas."

"It's cool that you get to work," I remarked. "There aren't many jobs for teenagers in Saddle Pass. Even if I found one, my parents would be scared that my grades would suffer."

She nodded. "Dad's that way too. That's why I mainly help out on weekends—and more when it's a school break. Dad usually opens up the place, but a couple of weeks ago I begged to work mornings instead of evenings so I could spend more time with my boyfriend, Wade."

"You have a boyfriend?" I tried my best to sound cool and calm, but the prickles of insecurity inside me suddenly felt like a T. rex chomping on my intestines.

"*Had* a boyfriend. Past tense. Dead and buried . . . or so I wish. Last week I found out Wade had been two-timing me with a girl in Yorba Linda. I knew he wasn't the love of my life, but I still felt violated and humiliated, you know?"

I did know. All too well. I considered telling her about Tasha and my own rude surprise, but I decided not to. At least, not yet. If I had any chance at all of coming across as a cool super-dude with Halle, I couldn't let her find out about my past failures.

"Tough break. He sounds like a loser."

"Yeah," she said quietly, staring down at the counter.

Just then the door opened and a college-aged couple walked in.

"Whoops," she muttered. "Time to get grinding."

"Yeah. I should get going," I said. I decided to head back to the condo rather than stand around like a dork as she worked. Sean was probably wondering where I was anyway.

"What? Already? I haven't even gotten your coffee yet."

"I know, but you're going to get busy here, and I need to go . . . do stuff."

"Oh, okay. Well, take a nap or something before your eyes completely recede into your skull." She flashed me a wry smile.

"Will do. Hey, you want to give me another beach jogging lesson tomorrow morning? I think

I have the hang of it, but I need to figure out how to avoid getting tons of sand in my shoes."

She laughed melodically and nodded. "As long as you promise to rest up."

"Sure thing," I replied, heading for the door.

"Oh, and Devin?"

"Yeah?"

"Next time try not to give me a concussion, okay?"

Five

Sean

TWO DAYS IN Newport Beach and all we had done was sit around the condo watching rental flicks and playing cards with Uncle Gary. For me it was cool not having to worry about my folks or school or a certain ex-girlfriend. Also, I'd been there a few times before and had already done the touristy stuff. But Devin, I could tell, was getting antsy.

He wasn't around when I woke up, so I figured he went running. That dude had to be the most disciplined high-school jock I knew.

I chomped on some strawberry Pop-Tarts and flipped through the TV channels. Nothing was on but a lame game show where people scream and jump up and down over winning a microwave. I switched off the set and started hobbling around the condo, trying to figure out what to do. I had already read all the sports magazines, there was no one around to play cards with, and Gary had apparently gotten rid of his Nintendo set. No wonder Devin went out. This place was losing its appeal fast.

Of course, there was Alex. Maybe I could see what she was up to. Images of her face started flooding my brain like a slide show. Her sultry eyes, perfect teeth, hair so glossy I had to stop my hands from touching it.

Get a grip, Foster! I scolded myself. *You're just bored. Do something!*

A note from Gary lay on the dining-room table. It read, *I'll be back early today. Make yourself at home, homey!—Uncle Scary.*

Something was up with Gary. He seemed different since we got here, sort of jumpy and distracted, not at all the laid-back party guy he usually was. Then there was the whole business of his condo. No more stereo, water bed, or Nintendo? I asked him about it, and he just stuttered that he had needed some extra cash recently and was tired of those things anyway. It didn't make sense, though. Gary had just been promoted at work, and he was driving a new forty-thousand-dollar truck. He'd even hired a cleaning woman.

I once saw this movie about these people who sold all their stuff and sat around on pillows meditating, trying to simplify their lives and get in touch with their spiritual side. Maybe this was a California craze Gary was slowly slipping into. Somehow, though, I couldn't see Gary sitting cross-legged on the floor, chanting to himself.

I wandered into the kitchen to get the box of Pop-Tarts. The place was a mess. Greasy plates and pans left over from the Sean Burger lunch, food-crusted knives and spoons, and a row of empty aluminum cans that needed to be recycled were all scattered about. I wondered when the cleaning lady was going to come by. *Oh, well,* I thought, *I might as well do it. There isn't squat to do around here anyway.*

It didn't take me long to rinse everything and load it into the dishwasher. After I was done, I couldn't find any powdered soap like we use at home, so I used some of the dishwashing liquid that was sitting next to the sink. Then I headed for the bathroom to shower and dress. I figured when Devin got back, I'd suggest a trip to the pier or something, play tour guide for a day.

When I returned from the bathroom, I couldn't believe my eyes. A pile of soapsuds several inches high covered the kitchen floor. As I stood there wondering what had happened, the bubbly mountain got bigger as more and more suds poured out of the sides of the dishwasher.

Mop! I need a mop! I thought, but a quick search of the place showed I was out of luck. Meanwhile the bubbles kept growing like some sort of foamy creature. On an impulse I ran across the hall and knocked on Alex's door.

"Hi!" she said cheerfully when she opened the door. "How are you do—"

"Can I borrow a mop?"

Her eyebrows lowered. "That spatula not working out for you?"

"No, it's great, but, well, there's sort of a flood in my uncle's kitchen and—"

"What?" she exclaimed. Then she disappeared from the doorway, ran back with a mop and bucket, and raced across the hall to Gary's condo.

"Oh, my God!" she cried when she saw the mountain of bubbles. "What happened?"

"I don't know. I think I broke Gary's dishwasher. I guess I filled it kind of full, and I had to use dishwashing liquid since he was out of the powdered stuff, then I took a shower and—"

"You used dishwashing liquid?" She looked at me like I was her little brother, half disbelieving and half amused.

"Uh, yeah." I felt like a total dweeb. "I guess I better turn off the dishwasher before the suds reach the ceiling."

I started to wade into the foam, but Alex held me back. "Don't! It's real slippery, and you've got a hurt leg. Let me."

"I'll be okay," I said in an exasperated voice. I felt totally embarrassed as it was. Having her protect me would make me feel more pathetic.

"Don't be macho," she scolded. "You want to play football again, right?"

Before I could answer, she was off trudging through the bubbles.

"There," she said, turning the switch on the dishwasher. "Now hand me the mop and . . . *whoa!*" Suddenly her feet slid out from under her and she ended up on the floor with bubbles up to her shoulders. I couldn't help it; I started laughing. This was like something you'd see on a crazy sitcom.

"Stop it!" she said, but she was laughing too.

"Here, let me help you." I took a couple of steps toward her and held out my hand. She grasped it firmly and I started to pull her up. But the next thing I knew my feet lost all traction and I slid in her direction like a downhill skier. She fell again with a *splat,* and I plopped down right next to her.

"Thanks a lot," she said mockingly, throwing a handful of bubbles onto my head.

"Hey!" I exclaimed, scooping some up and tossing them at her.

We continued sliding around on the kitchen floor, laughing and flinging soapsuds onto each other. By the time we stopped, the suds had melted down to a white froth, and most of the water had been sopped up by our clothes.

"Well, there's not much left to mop up," she pointed out, sounding out of breath.

"Nope," I agreed, unable to stop staring at her. Her eyes were still twinkling mischievously, her clothes and the ends of her hair were damp, and a smattering of suds clung to her shoulders and forehead. For some reason I thought about that goddess we'd studied in mythology—the one that just rose up out of the sea foam one day. The goddess of beauty and love.

Don't go there, Foster, I ordered myself. *Don't go getting all mushy.*

"How are you feeling?" she asked softly.

"Fine! I'm all right," I answered, almost shouting at her. I was afraid she might've seen the dopey stare on my face and thought I'd fallen for her. "I just noticed you have some bubbles in your hair. That's all."

"I meant your leg. Did you hurt it when you fell? Could you have made your injury worse?" Her eyebrows were all bunched up with worry, making little creases on her forehead. I instantly felt like a jerk for overreacting.

"I'm okay. I think my rear end took most of the impact," I said. "Thanks a lot for your help. Can I pay you back somehow? How about a soda?"

"Actually, I just finished making lunch when you knocked," she explained. "You want to come over and have some? It's just leftovers, but we have a ton."

"Well, I don't know. . . ." I felt like I was the rope in a tug-of-war game. Half of me really wanted to go, while the other half was telling me not to.

"Oh, come on," she said tilting her head and smiling. "It's too dangerous for you to stay in this kitchen anyway. Besides, you can help me with the dishes afterward."

She flashed me a playful smirk and tilted her head again. I was quickly getting yanked over to the "go for it" side.

"Okay, sure. I'll come over. Provided I can stand up." I scooted over by a cabinet and carefully pulled myself up to a standing position.

"Nicely done," Alex said, clapping. Then she cautiously stood up and walked toward me. "I'm going to go change clothes. I guess I'll—*whoops!*" Again her shoes slipped on the slick floor, but this time instead of falling backward, she fell forward . . . and into my arms.

Alex slowly lifted her head and looked at me. Wisps of her hair had fallen across her face, and our noses were only an inch or two apart. We were both trembling, but I told myself it was only because we were cold and wet.

"Nice catch," she said, blushing.

"Well, I *am* a wide receiver."

"Right. Hey! That better not be a crack about my weight or anything!" She pulled away and raised one eyebrow.

"I promise it isn't. But be glad I didn't do a victory dance and spike you."

She whacked me playfully on the shoulder and turned for the door. "See you in a few minutes," she called before walking out.

Once she left, I started to wig out. What the heck was I doing, agreeing to eat lunch with her? That's a textbook play formation for first dates. I was supposed to be avoiding anything *remotely* feminine . . . and Alex was like the gold standard for females.

It's not a date, I told myself as I carefully crossed the kitchen. *It's only . . . free food.* And anyway, she'd said her brother had really gotten a kick out of me. I'd be cheering the poor kid up. A good deed for the holidays.

I quickly changed clothes, combed my hair, and headed over to their condo. It was already after eleven, and I was afraid Devin might show up at any second. Luckily he didn't.

"Come on in," Alex called after I knocked on her door.

I let myself into the place and followed the drool-inducing smells all the way to the kitchen/dining area. The table was already set, and Alex was putting a platter of some hearty-looking chicken-and-rice dish on the table.

"Hi!" came Gabriel's voice from behind me. "You wanna see my new shoes? I got the kind with the air in the bottoms—the ones that make you jump good. I saw some cool black-and-white ones, but Grandma said they were too expensive. These were cool too, but they don't have the lights or that boomerang thing on the sides."

The kid was talking faster than I could process it. It was cute, though.

"Both of you, come and eat. It's getting

cold," Alex ordered, motioning to the chairs on either side of her.

We sat down and started to dig in. Or I did, rather. Gabriel just kept chatting on and on about the big arcade at the mall; his friend Tony, who can turn his eyelids inside out; how dogs supposedly can find crabs with their noses; and whether or not the Pirates of the Caribbean ride at Disneyland has a real buried treasure in it.

"Hey, Sean," Gabriel continued without taking a breath, "did ya know that when Alex was little, she used to be scared of clowns? Yeah, she would scream at the circus. She also used to say Santa Clock instead of Santa Claus. And she wouldn't eat nothing but Cheetos."

"All right! That's enough!" Alex exclaimed. "Gabriel, you need to stop talking for a second and eat. Otherwise you won't have enough energy to tell Sean all *your* embarrassing stories."

Gabriel rolled his eyes and lifted his fork to his mouth.

"This is really good," I remarked. "My mom makes some sort of rice-and-chicken dish, only it's not as spicy. What do you call this?"

"Arroz con pollo."

"Oh. Cool." The dish's name sounded as exotic as it tasted. "What does that mean?"

"Rice with chicken." She giggled.

"Oh."

"My grandpa used to have chickens," Gabriel put in. "He had a farm, and we'd go visit him.

He let me sit on his lap when he drove the tractor, and we could go fishing on his pond. One time I caught a fish. I don't like to eat fish, do you? It's smelly. One time I had a bone in my throat, and I coughed and coughed. Mommy was yelling, and Alex said my face was purple."

As he rambled on, Alex flashed me a sympathetic look. I smiled at her to let her know that everything was cool.

By the time I finished my third helping, Gabriel finally finished his first—with lots of goading from Alex. When he announced he was done, I stood up and began clearing away the plates and forks.

"Hey, whatcha doing?" Gabriel asked.

"The dishes. Your sister helped me out today, so now I'm going to help her."

"I was only joking about that," Alex said. She stood up and tried to grab the plates from my hands. "You don't actually have to do them."

"I want to."

"But you're a guest."

"So what?"

"Hey, Sean, you wanna see my football card collection?" Gabriel asked, tugging on my elbow. "Come on. I got lots, but I don't got Jerry Rice yet."

"Sure, after I'm finished."

"Oh, go on," Alex said, taking the plates from me. "I'll just rinse these and put them in the dishwasher. *I* know how to operate it."

Ouch.

I followed Gabriel to his room and oohed and ahhed appropriately at his card collection. He only had a couple dozen, but he held each one up like it was priceless, telling me each athlete's name and important stats as if I were new to it all.

"This guy's a wide receiver too," Gabriel told me. "Look how he's way up in the air." He handed me a card that showed Alvin Harper jamming the ball over the goalpost. "Can you do that?"

"Sometimes. When I'm in top form."

"Maybe you and me could go sometime to see a game. They got Raiders and Chargers tickets on sale. They used to have the Rams, but they're not here anymore."

"Gabriel." Alex's voice came from the doorway. She looked from me to Gabriel with a worried expression on her face. "I, um, need you to take out the trash."

"Aw, man. Can't I do it later?"

"No. Hurry up and do it now, or you'll forget and be in trouble."

"Why do you always make me do that when I'm having fun?" he whined, stomping toward the door.

"Hey, Gabriel," I called after him. "I need to be going too. But thanks for showing me your cards, dude. You got a cool collection."

"Thanks! I'll see you later, okay?" he said, then disappeared around the corner.

"Listen, Sean," Alex began in a low, serious voice. "Be careful what you say around Gabriel. I think it's wonderful that he's really opened up to you. It's been so long since he's been that way." She paused for a second and looked off toward the corner of the room. Tears began to well up in her eyes. "But since you're only here visiting for a little while, try not to promise anything you can't keep, okay?"

I was blown away by the emotion in her voice. I followed her gaze to a framed photo on Gabriel's dresser. It was the picture of an older man with graying hair, the same unusual eyes as Alex, and a smile as broad as his shoulders.

"Don't worry," I said, looking back to her and resisting the urge to put my arm around her. "I know I can't promise anything. I'm only here for a couple of weeks, and I'll probably be busy the whole time hanging with Uncle Gary and my buddy Devin—doing guy stuff, you know?"

She met my eyes, looking a little startled. "Oh, uh, yeah. Of course. Well, I hope we get to see you sometimes at least."

Again I felt the wrestling match going on inside me. "Maybe. We'll probably see each other in the halls and stuff. And I need to give you your spatula back anyway. That is, when it's safe to enter Gary's kitchen again."

She laughed, shaking her head. I noticed that even though her hair was now dry, it had a watery sheen to it. Before I went all weak again, I wrenched my eyes away from her and started to walk down the hall toward the front door.

"Well, thanks a lot for helping me out. And thanks for lunch. It was top-notch," I called to her over my shoulder.

"No problem."

I paused as I placed my hand on the doorknob and turned for one last look. "Well . . . I'll see you around."

"Yeah. Sure," she said. "See you around."

I sat in Gary's condo, trying to erase the mental image of Alex as she'd stared shyly into my eyes and shivered in my arms. I couldn't even think about going into the kitchen without an instant replay of her going off in my mind.

When Devin finally got back from his run (I swear the dude must have jogged to San Francisco and back), I suggested we go to the harbor for a while. But he said he had a headache and excused himself to go take a nap.

I was slouched on the couch, watching Oprah Winfrey and thinking about Alex, when Gary came home.

"Hey, Sean-man. Told you I'd be back early. How do you fellas feel about getting some pizza? They make a mean thin-crust Canadian bacon with pineapple at this place downtown."

"Sounds good," I said, grateful for the interruption in my thoughts. "But we have to wait for Dev to wake up. He was feeling tired and went to take a nap."

"He's asleep, huh? Hmmm. You boys must be up to some wild sightseeing while I slave away at work." Gary walked into the kitchen, pulled a glass down from the cupboard, and opened the fridge. Suddenly he stopped, looked down, and turned around in a slow circle.

"Did somebody clean the floor in here?" he asked.

I started to panic a little, wondering what I should tell him. "Uh, yeah. I did. It was pretty gross, and I figured it was the least I could do to pay you back for your hospitality. Besides, that maid you have is lame. It looked like the place hadn't been cleaned in weeks."

"Oh, yeah," Gary responded, looking preoccupied. "You're right. I've been thinking about going with another service."

I nodded, glad that the subject had been changed.

"Well, thanks a lot for mopping," Gary remarked. "Hey, wait a minute. I don't have a mop. How the heck did you clean the floor? On your hands and knees?"

"Uh, yeah," I mumbled as a slow-motion teleplay of the morning's events began rolling in my mind. "Something like that."

Six

Devin

THE NEXT MORNING I joined Halle for another jog. I met her on the beach again and stretched with her (this time at a safe distance), then we took off toward the pier. Occasionally we'd chat about the scenery or one of us would remark on something we passed. Mainly, though, we just ran. What amazed me was how well we matched each other's rhythm, stride by stride, as if we were toys that had been wound up simultaneously.

Yet as perfect as it was with Halle, I told myself I wouldn't hang around the coffee shop talking with her afterward. I was worried about Sean. For the last two days he'd done nothing but watch TV. I doubted he'd even left the condo at all. And the evening before, when I got on his case about his hair sticking up all funny and reached over to muss it up, it felt stiff and bunchy, as if he'd taken a shower but forgot to rinse the shampoo out of his hair. I mean, I knew he was still upset about Jo Beth breaking up with him, but I was beginning to wonder if he might be clinically depressed.

I doubted he would do anything crazy—Sean's way too tough for that. Still, I was afraid he might be more despondent than he let on.

"You seem more rested today," Halle said as we ran down the beach, veering to avoid a surge of ocean water. "Did you get a good night's sleep?"

"Yep."

"Eat breakfast?"

"Yes, Mom."

"What did you eat?"

"Frosted Pop-Tarts."

"Yuck! Is that all? You can't manage something better? A poached egg or whole-grain cereal?"

"Well, it isn't my place, and I didn't include my box of Wheaties when I packed to come here. Also, it's really weird, but there's no room service at the condo. Should I call city hall and complain?"

"Oh, you're funny," she responded. "So why don't I come up and meet you in that fancy condo some morning? We could have breakfast together before we go run. I make a mean omelette."

"Er, well. That sounds great, but . . . see, the place really isn't all that fancy. In fact, it's sort of a dump. My friend's uncle, the guy who owns the place, he's a total bachelor. He barely has any furniture even, let alone kitchen utensils." I paused to take a breath and ran a hand through my hair. "Also, my buddy is, um, not feeling well lately. I wouldn't want to disturb him."

"Oh, right. You mentioned he likes to sleep late."

"Yeah. He has to . . . on account of the medication he takes."

"Jeez, it sounds serious. I hope he's okay."

"He will be. He just has to, uh, stay in bed for the next several days."

"Now I know why you're always out here by yourself. Must be a real bummer for your friend—getting sick on vacation."

"Yeah."

By this time we were only a few yards away from the pier. Halle slowed to a walk and said, "It's really great running with you. It seems to go a lot faster."

"We definitely run well together."

"We do. And I've never been able to find someone who can run with me. Wade tried it a couple of times, but he couldn't handle it." Her eyebrows lowered and her hands balled up into fists. "Nope, I think fishing would be a better sport for ol' Wade. He's certainly good at stringing people along."

I hated that guy even though I'd never met him. I even hated his name. *Wade.* He sounded like a Brad Culpepper—some slick dude who attracts girls like crazy but never treats them right.

"I really appreciate you telling me about beach running," I said, trying to change the subject. "It's much more fun than pounding the pavement."

"Yeah. I need to confess something, though. I have no idea how to keep the sand from getting into your shoes. It sure gets itchy." She propped her left foot onto the pier and rolled down her sock to scratch.

"What's that?" I asked, pointing to her foot. There, right above her ankle, was a tiny tattoo of a turtle.

"What? Oh, that. Yeah, I got it last summer while visiting friends in San Francisco. I sort of collect turtles. Ever since I was a little girl, I've been fascinated by them. I have tons of them at home, all over my room."

"Real turtles?"

"Oh, no. Stuffed ones and sculpted ones and charms for my bracelet. Not to mention this permanently inked sketch one on my leg. Dad wasn't too happy about it."

I looked down at the tattoo. Normally I thought tattoos were for sailors or people with masochistic tendencies. But on Halle it just looked right, accenting her already perfect leg like a jewel.

We stretched out a bit, then walked down to the coffee shop. Halle began her usual routine of opening up the place, and I helped her out by filling up the sugar canisters, pouring coffee beans into the large electric grinder, and getting a big box of Sweet'n Low packets off a high shelf.

"Hey! I almost forgot to tell you!" Halle exclaimed as she added a roll of paper to the cash register. "There's a big beach party tonight that Bowman told me about. It should be a blast. You want to come? You might find your perfect moment there."

"I'd really like to, but I can't." Boy, did I want to. "I'm sorry. I have to get back and take care of my buddy Sean."

"Oh, right. Well, you want to give me your phone number? There's going to be all sorts of Christmas festivities going on the next couple of days. Maybe you and your friend could come to some of them—if he's up to it."

"I—I would, but . . . see, the phones aren't working where we're staying."

"Really?"

"Yeah. Um, everyone is really upset about it, but apparently the phone company said it'll be a few days until they fix everything." I was amazed at how easily the lies were coming now.

"Wow," she said, scratching her head. "There was a small tremor close to here a few days ago. I wonder if it has something to do with that?"

I shrugged. "Beats me. But why don't you give me your number? I could call you from a pay phone."

"Okay, sure." She pulled a napkin from a nearby canister, scribbled down some numbers, and handed it to me. "I know you're busy, but I hope we can keep meeting each other for a jog or whatever."

"Me too," I said, folding the napkin and placing it in my pocket. "Well, I need to get going now."

"Already? Oh, come on. At least take an orange juice for the road. Especially considering the lousy breakfast you had."

I smiled. "Okay. Hey, this time I'll even pay." I opened my wallet to take out a couple of dollar bills.

"Ooh. Who's that? She's pretty." Halle craned her head around and stared at my open wallet. A picture of Tasha grinned at us through the display pocket. I'd forgotten to take it out.

"Um, uh, nobody. She's a friend of the family."

"Really?" Halle asked with a wry smile. "Let me see the back. I bet something mushy is written there."

She was right. Tasha had scrawled *To Sweetcheeks* (a nausea-inducing nickname she'd created for me), *hugs and kisses, your Hunny Bunny* (an alias she'd devised for herself that I could never, ever bring myself to say). No way was I going to ruin my tough image by letting Halle see that.

"Come on. Hand it over," she ordered, tugging at the wallet.

"No! What are you doing, mugging me?"

"Aw, isn't that cute! You're blushing!"

So much for looking tough. I could feel my cheeks baking like a couple of turnovers. I hated that about myself. Whenever I get embarrassed, it's like all the blood in my body pools at the sides of my face. Tasha thought it was "cute" too. Maybe that was the basis for her wonderful nickname.

Thinking about Tasha dredged up the humiliation and frustration I'd been trying to keep in check these past few weeks. Without meaning to, I angrily wrenched my arm away from Halle, causing her to smack her chin on the counter.

"Ow!" she yelled, looking shocked.

"Oh, I'm sorry!" I exclaimed, snapping out of my temporary rage. I reached over and gently rubbed the perfect point of her chin. "Are you okay? I really didn't mean to hurt you. I was just . . . just . . ."

"No, *I'm* sorry, Devin," she said, placing her hand on my arm. "I shouldn't have teased you like that. I was being a brat. I guess I was just curious and got carried away."

"Well, I shouldn't have overreacted."

"Well, you wouldn't have if I'd respected your privacy."

"Well, maybe I should be less private."

"Maybe you should." She grinned at me from across the counter, her green eyes flashing like traffic lights. *Go!* they seemed to be saying.

I leaned forward and gently lifted her face toward mine. But just as my lips started to descend, the front door burst open, causing us both to jump apart.

"Whoa, it's getting hot!" the newcomer announced. He was an incredibly tall, skinny guy with a long blond ponytail and fuzzy goatee.

He was wearing a baggy T-shirt, baggy plaid shorts, and sandals that looked like they came from biblical times.

"Wh-What are you talking about, Bowman?" Halle asked. It was her turn to blush.

He looked from her to me and back. "Uh . . . the weather? Don't you think it's, like, a scorcher today?"

"Oh, yeah," Halle said, regaining her cool. "It's beautiful out."

"At last!" Bowman sang out, heading for the counter. "This is more like it. Gotta hand it to California. I love the weather, man. Well, not the weatherman, but the weather. You know."

He stood next to Halle, bobbing his head up and down to some unheard song.

"Um, Bowman? I'd like you to meet Devin." Halle motioned to me.

"Hi," I said.

"Yeah," Bowman responded. He pointed his index finger at me and smiled. "I like this dude." Then he turned and walked into the back room.

"How can he say that?" I whispered. "He just met me."

Halle shrugged. "Bowman says he can size people up in a second. He can see their aura or feel their vibes or something."

"Oh." I figured the guy must crank his bass way too high. I glanced at my watch. "Well, I gotta run."

"Do you really have to? I thought we could, you know, talk some more."

"I'd like that, but I have to get back. There's some . . . things my friend and I have to do." *Like eat popcorn and watch* Matlock *reruns,* I thought glumly.

"You know something?" she asked, tossing me a container of orange juice. "You are one mysterious guy, Devin."

All right! I thought as I smiled back at her. *It's working!*

I'd just turned the doorknob to the condo when the door suddenly flew open in front of me. Gary stood there looking wide-eyed and worried.

"Oh, Devin," he said. "It's you."

"Hey, buddy," Sean called from the couch as I walked in. "You're back early today. You must be getting faster, huh?"

"Um, yeah. A little," I said, searching his eyes for any hidden sarcasm. "And I didn't go as far today."

"You know, it really is a gorgeous day. I was just telling Sean you guys should go stroll along the pier or something, take in some of our California sunshine." Gary motioned to the front door like a game-show model would gesture to a grand-prize automobile.

"Um, the pier?" I echoed.

"Yeah, have you been down there yet? It's really cool. Let's go," Sean said.

"But—but you really shouldn't be walking around too much on your bum leg," I pointed out.

"Nah, it's fine," Sean replied.

"And, um, I just got back from a hard run. I don't know if I'm really up for it."

Sean cocked his head at me and scrunched up his eyes in puzzlement. "Okay . . . why don't we wait an hour or so, then go. Don't worry, we'll take it easy—just walk down the pier, maybe grab a cup of coffee."

"No!" Gary and I exclaimed at the same time. We exchanged surprised looks.

"It's just that, well, I need you guys to make yourself scarce real soon," Gary explained. "See, uh, the cleaning-service woman is coming by, and we really should get out of her way."

"Oh, no prob, Scary. Why didn't you say so? I'm glad you're finally gonna get your money's worth out of her." Sean lifted himself off the couch and stretched his arms. "Come on, Schaub. Let's go sit on the beach for a couple of hours. Catch ourselves a Christmas tan."

"Sounds great!" I said, relieved he'd dropped the idea of the pier. *That* could have turned into a mess. I pictured him insisting we go into Blinkers for a cappuccino. Then when Halle called me by name and referred to our morning jogs, Sean would realize I violated his sacred pact and send me flying back to Saddle Pass—without an airplane!

We packed up a blanket, a couple of sodas, and some magazines, then headed outdoors to the beach. When I took off my running shoes in the sand, I was surprised at how warm it felt under my feet.

"Is this cool or what?" Sean opened his arms wide and breathed in the ocean air, like a Ray-Ban-wearing monarch surveying his kingdom. "I bet everyone back home is wearing coats and keeping their faucets dripping at night so their pipes don't freeze."

We hiked down the beach a ways and spread out the quilt. All around us people were running around in shorts and swimsuits. I couldn't believe it would be Christmas in just three days.

While I read magazines, Sean sat back on his hands and stared out at the ocean. He seemed to be brooding over something. I would have bet anything he was still smarting over Jo Beth. Why couldn't he just snap out of it? I guess he'd never had to deal with rejection before. It probably threw his macho outlook on life into a complete tailspin.

"Hi, there," a voice came from above.

I looked up and saw two feminine outlines silhouetted against the sun. One of them looked very pregnant.

"Uh, hi," I answered, wondering why they had approached.

The two figures stepped around to the front of the blanket, moving out of the sun's glare. They looked like they were about our age. Both of them were wearing incredibly small bikinis, and the one who I'd originally thought looked pregnant was actually carrying a volleyball in her hands.

"My name's Michelle," the one in the orange bikini said.

"I'm Daria," said the one in pink.

"Nice to meet you. I'm Devin." I looked over at Sean, waiting for him to take his cue. Instead he cast his glance to the sky. "Um, and this is Sean."

"I love your accent!" Michelle squealed. "Where are you from? Texas?"

"Oklahoma," I corrected.

"We were just trying to put together a game of volleyball," Daria said to Sean, twisting her big toe in the sand next to him. She was eyeing him with that same hormone-crazed look most girls cast in his direction. "Do you play?"

"No," he responded curtly.

"Okay, then. How about a swim?" Michelle asked.

"No! My buddy and I just want to hang out by ourselves and chill. Can't you leave us alone?"

"Fine!" Daria snapped. "You don't have to be such a jerk! What's your problem anyway?"

"You're my problem!" Sean responded as they retreated down the beach.

I couldn't believe it. Had he actually banished two good-looking, scantily-clad females from his presence?

"Jeez, Sean! They were just trying to be nice."

"Man, we can't go anywhere without girls coming around and bugging us," he grumbled.

Speak for yourself, I thought.

"People get too spazzed out over finding a girlfriend or boyfriend," Sean continued to rant. "Like this morning, I turned on the TV and all the talk shows were yammering on about how to find love at the grocery store, or super-makeovers to land a lover, or men who love too many women. Everything was love this or love that. It made me want to puke."

"Mmmm," I replied, trying to match the sourness in his voice.

"You know, if we want our grand plan to work, we need a couple more ground rules," he announced.

"What sort of rules?" I asked hesitantly.

"No hanging out at places where we're likely to meet girls. And no mentioning the *L* word."

Great, I thought glumly as I stared back at him in disbelief. *While we're at it, how about banning the color pink or prohibiting anything hourglass shaped?* He had really gone off the deep end.

I thought about Halle. Sean would lose all sanity if he found out about her. If I valued my dull yet safe existence, I needed to stay away from her altogether.

Somehow, though, I knew I wouldn't.

Seven

Sean

ALL I WANTED was to be able to think straight. My mind seemed all scrambled lately, like a puzzle someone had busted up.

Two days ago, when I had lunch with Alex, I knew I was getting all weak around her. I could feel myself being reeled in like a fish whenever she looked at me with her dark, almond-shaped eyes.

Then, later that same day, my folks called from Colorado. My mom spoke to me first, asking all sorts of mom stuff, like whether I'd been eating right and taking care of my knee. Afterward Dad told me about his snowboarding adventures. He bragged that he'd managed to make it all the way down the slope that day without falling.

"Except he went down backward!" Claire's voice yelled in the background.

Eventually Claire grabbed the phone. She made me sick talking about the fresh powder on the slopes, the food at the lodge restaurant, the great hot tubs. Plus Dev and I were staying just outside Hollywood and *they* were the ones running into movie stars. The best Vail vacation yet, and I was three states away, chewing on a cold piece of pizza and watching lame Christmas specials on TV.

"Oh, and I saw Jo Beth today," Claire went on.

My stomach suddenly felt as if Freddy Krueger was raking his talons over it. "Really?" I responded, trying to sound matter-of-fact. I silently hoped that Claire had seen her hanging upside down from the ski lift.

"Yep. She asked about you and said to tell you hi."

"How nice. Well, tell her I said break a leg."

"Sean," Claire scolded in her know-it-all voice. "That's what you tell performers when they're about to go onstage. *Not* people on a ski vacation."

Duh. I meant exactly what I said.

After hanging up, I started to feel really bummed out. There was Jo Beth having the time of her life, and I wasn't any better off than I'd been back home. But then I realized I hadn't really given my plan a chance to work. My first morning here I'd met Alex and hadn't been able to think straight since.

It was supposed to be easy: spend two weeks away from women and get my head on straight again. But getting away from girls was harder than I'd thought it would be. When Dev and I went down to the beach, there were girls everywhere—it was like getting blitzed by the 49ers defense. Unfortunately sitting around the condo—the female forbidden zone—was no fun either. All I ended up doing was daydreaming.

Before he went to take a shower, Dev said he wasn't going to go running today. I figured we could go to the movies. Just when I started flipping through the theater listings, there was a knock at the door. I opened it to find Gabriel grinning up at me.

"Hey, you wanna go with us to Dizzyland today?" he asked.

"Disneyland?"

"No, *Dizzy*land. It's smaller, but it has roller coasters. Alex promised she'd take me since I helped her with a bunch of stuff. You wanna go?"

In the background I could hear Devin turning off the water in the shower. He would be out any minute.

"Thanks, dude, but I don't think so. I've got a lot to do today."

"Aw, come on. Please? We won't stay a long time. Alex isn't any fun to go with because she's scared of all the cool rides. But I know you aren't scared of anything."

Devin was whistling in the bathroom. How would I explain it if he walked out and saw Gabriel standing here pleading with me? I'd have to tell him about how we met. Then I'd probably have to explain about Alex. Still, short of slamming the door on the kid's face, I couldn't figure out how to get rid of Gabriel fast.

"Okay, okay. I'll go. But only for a little while."

"All right!" he whooped.

"I need a few minutes here, then I'll come over to your place. Got it?"

"Okay," he said, bouncing happily in his new sneakers. "See ya!" Then he skipped across the hall.

Devin came out of the bathroom just as I was shutting the front door.

"Did someone knock?" he asked.

"Oh, uh, yeah. You know, some charity. I gave them a couple of dollars to help out a needy kid." That wasn't too far from the truth.

"You're full of the Christmas spirit," he said, smiling skeptically at me. "So, tell me. What do you have planned for us today?"

"Hey, listen, Dev," I said. "I need to go someplace this morning. Can we hang out later this afternoon?"

"Er, sure. No problem. Where are you going?"

"I can't tell you."

He raised his eyebrows suspiciously.

"It's like this," I said, quickly formulating a story in my head. "I need to go do some last-minute Christmas shopping—including your present. So I sorta need to go by myself."

"Gee, Sean, you don't have to get me anything."

"I know. But I want to."

Devin looked at me like I was one of those killer test questions we get in calculus all the time. Lately it seemed everyone was looking at me that way. My folks, Claire, Alex—even Gary on occasion. I wondered if all this stress was making me look as weird as I felt.

"Well . . . later, man," I said, opening the door and stepping into the hallway. "If I'm not back by lunchtime, help yourself to any of that canned stuff."

"Okay. See ya later."

I could see the confused look on Devin's face as I shut the door.

What do you think you're doing? I asked myself as I knocked on the Lopezes' front door.

Just when I thought my brain would melt from all the pressure, I now had two more problems to think about: figure out a way to be around Alex for several hours and not turn into a total wuss and locate a gift for Devin sometime before Christmas.

Alex opened the door and smiled sheepishly at me.

"I'm sorry, Sean. I had no idea he was going to sneak over there and ask you to come along. You don't have to if you don't want to. I *know* how whiny and persistent he can be."

Alex looked incredible in a flowery dress held up by two shoelace-thin straps. Everything about her was long and soft. Her short dress showed off her long bronzed arms and legs, and her hair draped over her shoulders and down her back like a silky cape.

"He *wants* to come, Alex. I didn't make him say yes. Did I, Sean?" Gabriel asked from behind her. Between his big pleading eyes and Alex's flirty sundress, all my defenses came crumbling down.

"No, you didn't. I want to come."

I decided I wasn't really cheating on our no-girls pact. It wasn't like I'd asked Alex on a date or anything. I was doing this for Gabriel's sake. Besides, it would be cool to get out somewhere and have fun—take my mind off all the stress I'd been dealing with.

Alex locked up the condo, and we all went downstairs. I practically sprinted past Gary's door to the elevator, just in case Devin decided to leave at the same moment.

We drove down the shoreline to an amusement park just a few minutes out of town. It looked like it had been there since the 1950s. The rides were all old-fashioned ones with loud motors, flashing lightbulbs, and tinny background music. I hoped someone had tightened the screws on everything recently.

Gabriel was already racing to the entrance as Alex and I stepped out of her car. "Come on!" he yelled. "Before the lines get long!"

The first ride we went on was the Haunted House. We all piled onto this incredibly tiny train that ran through the house. It was pretty lame—there were lots of plastic witches popping up and screeching, mummies with lightbulbs for eyes, and a vampire with one missing fang.

"This is lousy," Gabriel announced, turning around and kneeling in his seat. He sat in the first cab, followed by Alex, then me. Apparently word had gotten out about how stupid the ride was, because we were the only ones on it.

"Sit back down, Gabriel," Alex ordered.

He ignored her and looked at me. "This ride is for babies, right, Sean? There isn't anything scary in—*yaaaaah!*"

Because he was facing the back of the train, Gabriel didn't see the wall of rubber arms the train was heading for. The minute those wiggly hands hit him, he started screaming and shaking like Richard Simmons on a fire ant mound. Popcorn flew everywhere. It's a wonder he didn't fall off the train into the Headless Horseman's arms.

Alex and I looked at each other and lost it. We were still laughing by the time the train lurched back out into the sunshine.

"Oh, Gabriel, thank you," Alex said, wiping tears from her eyes. "That was excellent."

Gabriel's cheeks were bright red, and his face was knotted up in a scowl. "I wasn't scared. It just surprised me. That's all."

Alex didn't want to go on any of the really fast rides, so Gabriel and I rode the Hammer, the Tilt-A-Whirl, and the Zipper. He was having a blast, and by the time we got off the Zipper, he was laughing about the Haunted

House incident too, even giving me reenactments of how he'd spazzed out.

"Come on, Gabriel. Let's ride the carousel," Alex called when we joined up with her again.

Gabriel rolled his eyes at me. "See? She never wants to do the fast, scary stuff, and she makes me ride the baby rides."

"Oh, be quiet," Alex said. "You know you like it too."

"Be careful, Alex!" I shouted after them as they got on line. "Those horses look rabid! And I think I saw a scary clown get on!"

I sat down on a nearby bench and watched them. They chose two steeds side by side—Alex on the white one and Gabriel on the orange one. Gabriel kept looking over at me and rolling his eyes, but when the ride started up, I could tell by his smile that he really enjoyed it. And Alex looked totally stoked. Her eyes were all lit up like one of those Haunted House mummies, and she had this incredible smile on her face. I know it sounds kooky, but she was so sweet and gentle looking that for an instant she seemed like a little girl—younger than Gabriel, even. I couldn't take my gaze off her.

"How was it?" I asked when it was over. "That looked like a wild ride. Are you okay, or do you want to sit down for a little while and recover?"

"Enough!" Alex shouted, socking me on the chest.

"Hey, let's go on the roller coaster!" Gabriel

pleaded. "See? The line's pretty short."

"Oh, no! Not me! You guys go ahead." Alex sat down on the bench and waved her hands in protest.

"Aw, you're no fun," Gabriel whined. "Come on, Sean. Will you come with me? Please?"

"Sure," I replied. "Just promise me you'll stay in your seat on this one."

We ended up riding it twice. Gabriel really got into it. He was very proud of himself too. Apparently last year he was too afraid to ride it, but this year he was older and fearless.

"I got scared in the Haunted House, but that's just 'cause I didn't see the stuff coming," he explained. "Alex is scared of everything, though. But you aren't scared of nothing!"

"Yeah, well, that's because I have you here to protect me," I said, reaching over to mess up his already windblown hair.

He talked me into riding one more time, then we went looking for Alex.

"That was awesome!" Gabriel called out as we approached her. "You have to try it!"

"No way."

"Aw, go on," I urged.

"Come on, Alex," Gabriel whined. "I rode the merry-go-round. Now you gotta go on this one."

Glancing over at the roller coaster, Alex wrinkled up her forehead and bit her lower lip. We could tell she was caving.

"Well . . ." She looked over at me helplessly.

How could I resist a look like that? She was so impossibly cute. "Tell you what. I'll ride with you if you like," I offered.

She stared at me for a couple of seconds, then smiled weakly. "Okay. I guess. I mean, I suppose driving the LA freeway is probably more dangerous than this thing, right?"

Alex and I mounted the stairs to the entry platform while Gabriel stayed below, saying he wanted to "watch her freak out." The whole time we waited to get on, Alex wrung her hands nervously, wincing as we listened to the other passengers' screams.

Finally it was our turn. We got a car near the front. As we sat waiting, Alex leaned her head back against the seat and closed her eyes. Her knuckles were white where she gripped the safety bar, and her face was slowly losing color as well.

"Are you going to be okay?" I asked softly.

Alex slowly lifted her head and opened her eyes. "Sure," she said, smiling bravely. "I'll be fine."

Just then the cars lurched and we were off, climbing the first steep hill. When we reached the top, Alex took a deep breath and flashed me a frightened glance. A heartbeat later we were hurtling down the hill at breakneck speed. Instead of screaming or yelling out prayers, Alex grabbed hold of my right arm with both her hands and buried her face in my shoulder. For the rest of the ride she stayed like that. And I didn't mind one bit—she could've held on to me for rest of her life as far as I was concerned. Eventually, though, the train slowed, and we were chugging back to the entry platform. Alex relaxed her grip but still kept her head down.

"It's over now," I murmured into her ear. "Are you all right?"

Keeping hold of my arm, Alex raised her head and looked around. Her hair was blown back and her cheeks were flushed pink—she was as beautiful as ever. "Hey!" she exclaimed. "That wasn't half bad!"

She glanced up at me and smiled. My pulse racing, I wondered what it would be like to see that incredible smile every day. Her eyes were all wide and sparkly, just like when she was on the carousel, but her fingers were trembling against my arm. Or maybe I was the one trembling.

"Thanks," she said softly.

"No problem."

Her lips were a straight path down from mine—and only inches away. For a split second I felt myself falling toward her. The movement was slight, but it made me dizzy and shaky like no other ride had that day.

Suddenly, just as I could feel my breath mixing with hers, I stopped and pulled back. It was like my sanity broke through my clouds of emotion. *What do you think you're doing, Foster?* I thought. *You can't kiss her! It's totally off-limits.*

I sat there, frozen, trying to sort out my senses. My heart felt like a battering ram inside my chest and my stomach seemed to be doing calisthenics. I had never flipped out like this before. What the heck was going on?

It's the ride, moron, I told myself. *That gunky popcorn you ate just got all churned up by the roller coaster. That's all.*

I don't know if Alex realized I had almost kissed her or not, but she abruptly let go of my arm and sat up straight.

"I . . . I guess we should go find Gabriel," she said. Her cheeks looked even pinker, and she was nervously wringing her hands again.

"Uh, sure," I said.

By now the roller coaster had stopped at the platform and people were starting to get off. It felt funny to walk down the solid, unmoving wooden steps. My legs were all wobbly, like I had been out to sea for months.

"Whaddya think, Alex?" Gabriel asked as he bounced up and down on the sidewalk below. "Wasn't it cool?"

"Yes, it was. You guys were right. It really wasn't as horrible as I thought it would be." Her eyes met mine, and she gave me a small smile.

"So, did she lose it, Sean? You guys were too far away for me to tell. Did she freak out and go all crazy?"

"No, she didn't," I replied, smiling back at Alex.

But *I* almost did.

Eight

Devin

WHY IS IT that when you spend a lot of time worrying over something, it ends up being for nothing?

The night before I'd tossed and turned, wondering what to do about Sean. He really seemed depressed lately, and all I'd done was sneak around to see a girl. Some friend I was. By morning I had made up my mind. I was going to spend the whole day with Sean. No jogging, no slipping away to act cool around Halle, no thinking about my problems at all. Instead I would focus on cheering up my buddy.

At first Sean seemed pleased when I announced I had no plans for the morning. But when I came out of the shower, he had suddenly changed his mind and said he needed to do some stuff alone. He told me he had to do some

Christmas shopping and—here's the scary part—was looking for a gift for me.

Sean had never bought me a present before. For anything. On my birthday he says, "Live it up, dude!" and that's about it. His standard congratulatory response for a victorious track meet is, "Way to go, homey!" If I'm upset, he'll say, "Man, what a drag," and then offer to beat someone up for me. Sean's a good buddy—but he is definitely *not* the sentimental type. The fact that he was buying me a Christmas gift was further evidence of his decaying mental state. If I didn't intervene soon, he'd be taking up gardening by the time we got back home.

And I had another thing to worry about: I didn't have a present for him in return. So I decided to head down to the beach shops and look for something.

It was another incredibly beautiful day. Lots of people were out walking, skateboarding, and playing Frisbee. A young couple jogged past, and I couldn't help but think about Halle.

I had never felt this way about a girl before. Things were so easy with her. With Tasha everything seemed forced, as if we were reading lines in a romance movie . . . and a bad one at that. But with Halle I felt at ease. She was so friendly and straightforward, and I didn't have to burst a blood vessel trying to talk with her. Everything just naturally fell into place.

I wondered if I should open up to her more,

considering the way she'd been so forthcoming with me. But maybe my acting mysterious was the reason she seemed interested. Girls like a challenge, right? I decided to stick with my present strategy and continue holding back details. Plus I had to keep Sean and our whole anti-women pact under wraps anyway. It wasn't like I could suddenly let her in on my whole life.

When I reached the pier, I gazed at the shop windows, hoping something Sean-like would scream out at me. Nothing seemed right. A lime green portable CD headset? Nah, he always thought those things looked dorky. A psychedelic tie-dyed shirt with California Dreamin' written on it? Maybe in another life. An imported needlepoint pillow that read Love Is Real? Oh, he would hurt me bad. How about a boxed set of stories by Raymond Chandler? Nope. Sean would probably confuse him for one of the characters on *Friends*.

What do you give a guy who hates everything?

I stopped walking and sighed dejectedly. Three shops down I could see the violet-neon sign for Blinkers. Should I go in and look for Halle? It seemed silly not to since I was so close by. Then again, visiting Halle on the sly while Sean bought me a present seemed really low.

I was just about to head back to the condo when something in a display window caught my eye. A little ceramic box in the shape of a turtle sat on a glass shelf. It was beige with a shell made of little green stones. He seemed to be grinning at me from his perch.

An omen.

Before I had time to think, I went into the store and bought the box. I had the saleslady wrap it up really well in tissue paper so it wouldn't break. Then I slipped it into my pocket and headed over to Blinkers.

Halle and Bowman were behind the counter, talking, when I entered.

"I'm telling you, Scooby-Doo and Astro are related. They sound the same, and they look like the same breed."

"You're totally wired, Bowman. Quit slamming the espresso. Astro supposedly exists a couple of centuries in the future, and Scooby is straight out of the seventies. No way they're related."

"Well, maybe Astro is Scooby's descendant. Hey, yeah! And maybe Dino on *The Flintstones* is their ancient ancestor!"

"What about Underdog and Hong Kong Phooey?" I asked, walking up to the counter.

"Devin! Hi! I didn't see you there." Halle flashed me a huge smile, making her cheeks ball up like peaches.

Bowman rubbed his chin contemplatively. "No, Astro and Scooby are of the hound dog variety. Those dogs seem more like beagles."

"Don't start, Bowman," Halle warned. She turned toward me. "So, what brings you down here?"

"I don't know. I was in the neighborhood and thought I'd stop by."

"Great! I was just about to take my lunch break. Do you want to join me? I have to stay in here in case it gets busy, but we could sit and talk awhile."

"Sounds good."

"Can I get you something to drink? An orange juice? It's on me."

"Sure, thanks."

Halle tossed me a container of juice, took off her apron, and then disappeared into the back room.

See? Aren't you glad you came? I thought. I was standing there staring after her like some sort of crazed fan when Bowman suddenly jumped in front of my view.

"You better watch out!" he said.

"Huh? What?"

"You better not cry," he continued. "You better not pout. I'm telling you why. . . ." Bowman started dancing around like Snoopy, shuffling his sandaled feet and swinging his ponytail back and forth while he dried a glass with a dishrag. "Santa Claus is coming to town!"

Halle emerged from the back and rolled her eyes. "I'm officially on break now, Bowman," she yelled out over his song. "Holler if you need me. Or actually, just call my name, okay? The last time you hollered, you scared two customers into spilling their coffee."

"Gotcha," he said, saluting with his cup towel.

We sat down at a rear table that faced the window.

"This is a nice surprise," Halle said. "So, you've been hanging out on the pier?"

"Yeah—I was doing some Christmas shopping. It's not going too well, though."

"Yuck. I hate shopping—especially this late. Let me know if I can help you," she said, straightening her cap.

That gave me an idea. "Actually, you might be able to. I was thinking about what to get my buddy for Christmas, and the only thing he really seems to get into lately is football—especially the 49ers. Where'd you get your hat?"

"There's a sporting-goods store three blocks away from the beach. It's only about a ten-minute jog from here. Well, fifteen minutes for you, maybe." She raised an eyebrow teasingly. "I'll draw you a map before you go."

"Cool. Thanks a lot."

"Hey! What's this?" She pointed to a rectangular box sitting on top of the napkin dispenser.

I picked up the box and opened it. "Looks like someone left behind a deck of cards."

"What luck! Do you play?"

"Do I play? Poker comes as easy as breathing for me," I boasted, expertly shuffling the deck.

My background in card playing isn't exactly as cool as it sounds. I never associated with any sly, cigar-chomping card sharks or anything. Actually, my brother and I learned poker out of a book.

When your folks limit TV watching as much as mine, you tend to find lots of unusual hobbies.

"Well, deal me in," Halle said. "Let's play a few hands."

Neither of us had much money, so we decided to play for coffee beans. We started off with a couple of hands of five-card stud, both of which I won. Then Halle won a hand of five-card draw.

Outside, a Salvation Army Santa Claus was ringing a bell for donations. He must have been sweltering in that thick, red suit. Occasionally a weary-looking passerby would drop a few coins in the pan, but most of the people seemed too busy to stop.

"I'm really getting fed up with Christmas," Halle grumbled as she contemplated her hand. She looked so cute, frowning down at her cards with her hat turned around backward. "All it ends up being is a lot of stress and guilt. People kill beautiful trees, prop them up in their living rooms, and throw junk on them. Then they kill more trees so they can send schmaltzy cards and wrap presents for people they barely know. You know what I mean?"

"Er, yeah." I tapped the turtle box in the pocket of my sweats. I decided to wait awhile before giving it to her.

"Oh, I'm sorry. I guess I sound really cynical, don't I? It's just that a few terrible Christmases in the past have made me kind of sour on it all."

"It's all right," I said. I'd always thought

everyone looked forward to Christmas. It had never occurred to me that it could dredge up bad memories for some people.

Halle closed her eyes and shook her head, as if physically casting off a foul mood. "So, tell me. What does your family do for the holidays?"

"Oh, just the regular stuff. Grandma comes and bakes a ton of cookies. We eat a big meal Christmas Eve and then open all our gifts. Then on Christmas Day we get the stuff from Santa."

"Aw, how *cute!*" Halle cooed. "You still get gifts from Santa?"

I could feel my cheeks lighting up. *Clam up, dude,* my conscience—sounding amazingly like Sean—ordered. *Or you'll lose all your cool status.*

"Um, uh, no. I mean, not me. My brother does," I stammered. "He knows what's up, but he still wants to get the biggest haul he can."

"Sure. Scam 'em while you're able. I fold, by the way." She scooped up all the cards and started to shuffle. "Dad and I don't really go for the traditions. We usually work Christmas Eve. Then on Christmas Day we get each other gifts and all, but that's about it. He doesn't put pressure on me to see long-lost relatives or bake pies, so most of the time we end up getting together with friends."

"And do what?"

"Whatever. Play Trivial Pursuit, make nachos, or drive around and look at all the gaudy Christmas light displays. I'd made plans with Wade to do some fun stuff, but that got canceled when I found out about his . . . reindeer games." Halle's mouth twisted sideways in a sour grimace and an awkward silence descended on our conversation.

Him again! I wanted to ask Halle for his address and go stuff him down the nearest chimney, but before I could say anything, a harsh sound hit my eardrums.

"What's that noise?" I asked, craning my neck around. The racket was coming from the front counter. "Is it getting busy up there? Do you need to go work?"

"Nah. Bowman's just banging a couple of spoons and singing 'The Little Drummer Boy.' It *is* getting late, though. I better eat my lunch fast."

Halle placed her cards down on the table, reached into a paper sack, and started to unpack her lunch. She lifted the lid off a plastic foam container, revealing an exotic-looking noodle dish.

"What's that?" I asked.

"*Chapchae*—it's a Korean specialty. Would you like to try some?"

"Sure."

Halle stabbed a generous portion with her fork and reached across the table. "Open wide," she sang, depositing the glob in my mouth.

I expected it to taste like bland ravioli, but it was really spicy—and tasty. "Oh, man. It's incredible," I raved between chews. "I've never tried anything like this before."

"It is good. I eat lunch at that place all the time.

Hey! Why don't I take you there tomorrow?"

"Tomorrow's Christmas Eve. Will it be open?"

"Yup—they don't celebrate Christmas. Anyway, Christmas Eve is a big moneymaker for eating establishments."

"It is?"

"Sure. On account of all the late shoppers who are out and about. We're going to be open too, but I'm not scheduled to work until late afternoon. What about you? Do you have plans?"

"No, I don't think so." Gary had already said he would be really busy on Christmas Eve, so we had planned to do our celebrating Christmas Day. I didn't know if Sean had plans for us, though.

"Aw, come on. You have to eat, don't you? I know your friend is sick and all, but can't you get away for a little while?" She shone her green eyes on me like a cobra hypnotizing its prey. I was a goner.

"Why not?" I replied. I figured if Sean had plans for us, it wouldn't be until evening anyway. "I'm sure I can sneak out—I mean, go out for a while."

"Great! It's a date," she said. She picked up her cards but looked at me instead of her hand. "Or is it? A date, I mean."

I fought my blood pressure from rising to prevent my cheeks from igniting again. "I'd call it a date," I murmured as coolly as I could. My heartbeat was like a drumroll in my ears, but I somehow managed to keep a level gaze.

I felt superhuman. In a matter of days I'd

actually gotten a gorgeous girl to go out with me. I was new and cool—just like Sean. All I had to do now was mastermind a plan to get away from Sean tomorrow.

Halle grinned. "All right. I'll see your French roast bean and raise you two Sumatra and three Columbian Supremo."

"I'm in," I said, sliding over a handful of greasy beans. "In fact, I'll see your bet and double it." I stared steadily and confidently into her beautiful eyes. Like I said, I felt invincible.

"Okay, I'll see your wager. Now show me that hand. This oughta be good."

I shrugged and set down my cards. "All right. So I bluffed a little. All I have is a pair of jacks."

"I knew it!" she exclaimed happily. "I could see through that pitiful poker face. Read 'em and weep. Three sevens. As in I win, I win, I win."

"Aw, man. That's the last time I try to fake you out," I said, laughing. I didn't care about losing. I had won over Halle with the new, improved me. That was all that mattered.

"That's why I trust you, Devin," Halle remarked, scooping up the pot of beans. "Unlike Wade, you're a lousy liar."

Nine

Sean

*'T*WAS THE DAY *before Christmas, and all through the condo not a creature was stirring, not even a . . .*

I didn't even want to think of a word that rhymed with *condo.* I was so incredibly bored, I was making up stupid poems in my head. My life had never been this lame.

Gary was working until five, and Devin had left a little while earlier to mail some souvenirs to his folks. What a Boy Scout. I figured he'd be gone for a while. Christmas Eve at the post office was probably total chaos.

I could have given Schaub some grief about blowing me off to run errands, but I'd left him behind yesterday so I could supposedly do some Christmas shopping. Going to the amusement park with Alex and Gabriel had been the most fun I'd had in a long time. Still, I felt like a snake, knowing that my buddy had been sitting around alone in the condo.

Scratching my scalp and yawning, I slowly stood up from the couch—which seemed to be conforming to my body like a second skin these days. I couldn't believe I'd been so excited about coming here. How was I supposed to get my head straight when there was nothing to do but sit around and feel sorry for myself? Devin was always out running, and Gary . . . well, something was definitely up with him.

The night before I'd watched a cop drama on TV where this teenage dude was picked up for burglary. The kid had been stealing stuff and selling all his folks' belongings in order to get money for drugs. Could Gary be hocking his loot in order to afford a quick fix? That would explain all his missing belongings. And he'd been really jumpy and weird since we'd arrived.

"Foster, you're wigging out," I said aloud. "Gary's the last dude to go that route." Hey, *that* rhymed.

Augh! I have to get out of this place!

I decided to see Alex and Gabriel. I couldn't stand being alone any longer, and they were the only people I could hang with. Besides, Gabriel had a way of making me feel like a cool dude again. And Alex . . . well, she made me feel all sorts of things, but I wasn't going to think about that. I mean, it wasn't like I was going to ask her out or anything, right?

"Hey! You and Gabriel want to go get some ice cream or something?" I blurted when Alex opened up her door.

"Hi!" she said, cocking her head and smiling sweetly. "We'd love to, but we have company. Why don't you come in?"

Alex opened the door wider to let me inside. I was immediately greeted by the smell of something delicious and the noise of several people talking in Spanish. The scents and sounds grew stronger as she led me through the living room and into the kitchen. There, six people, including Gabriel, were gathered about the room, cooking. Some were stirring big pots, others were cutting up meat, and Gabriel was standing in front of the sink, shaking water off some kind of leaves.

"We're making tamales for our Christmas Eve dinner tonight," Alex explained. "Come and meet everyone."

Before I could protest, she pulled me into the middle of the room. At first everyone was too busy to notice me, but then Alex cleared her throat and said, "Hey, guys. I want you to meet Sean. He's Gary's nephew—Gary from across the hall."

The group collectively shouted "hellos" and "nice-to-meet-yous." Alex took me around the room and introduced me to each family member: her aunts Nina and Blanca, her uncle Michael, and her grandmother, or *abuelita,* as Alex called her. Then she pulled me over to a tall, dark-haired woman who was stuffing chile peppers into a blender.

"Sean, this is my mom. Mom, this is Sean."

"Pleasure to meet you," Mrs. Lopez said, grasping my hand. Just like Alex, she was a total babe—for a mom, I mean. Only she looked more like Gabriel with her round eyes and dark wavy hair. "Alex, did you bring some more lard like I asked?"

"Whoops, I forgot. Excuse me a sec," she whispered before walking off.

"Well, Sean, I've heard a lot about you," Mrs. Lopez said.

"Really? Yeah, well, Gabriel and I are good buddies." The little guy probably fogged up the windows talking about our amusement-park adventures.

"I meant from Alexandra." Mrs. Lopez put a hand on my shoulder. "She told me how you've been so kind. Poor girl has had to spend her entire school break baby-sitting Gabriel, and I know she's appreciated your coming around and livening things up for them. I appreciate it too."

She smiled at me, but her eyes looked really sad. I had no idea what to say, so I just stammered, "No problem. My pleasure." Mrs. Lopez patted my shoulder a couple of times and turned back to her mixing.

Alex had been telling her mom all about me?

About how I'd rescued her from the boredom and dementia of taking care of her little brother? Weird. And I thought she was the one always coming to *my* rescue.

I remembered seeing that same sad look her mother gave me on Alex's face. All those times I'd wanted to reach out and protect her, but I suddenly realized how strong Alex must have been to handle everything that had happened to her family.

Gabriel ran up to me and tugged on my arm. "Hey! You wanna come spread *masa* with me?"

"Do what?" I asked. All the noise and activity was making my head spin.

"Spread *masa*—dough. Come on, I'll show you. It's easy."

"Gabriel, leave Sean alone," Alex scolded as she walked back up with the lard. "He has better things to do than make a bunch of tamales with us."

No, I don't, I thought. Aloud I said, "That's okay. I don't have plans . . . until later, I mean. And I still owe you for the spatula and dishwasher save. What do you say I help out for a while, and we call it even?"

Alex smiled. "Sounds great. I'll get you an apron."

Gabriel pulled me over to the table and began a running commentary. "First you get a corn husk out of the water and shake it dry. Then you spread it with a layer of *masa*. After that you put in the meat and roll it up good. See?"

Seemed easy enough. But when I tried it, I

couldn't spread the doughy stuff too well. It kind of globbed together on the spoon and wouldn't come off. Eventually Alex sat down with us and noticed my fumbling.

"Don't press down too hard. You need to glide it on smoothly, like frosting. Here, I'll show you." She grabbed my right hand in hers and gently distributed an even layer of the dough over the husk.

I tried to pay attention, but I couldn't stop staring at her hands. They were slender with long delicate fingers, so I expected her to have a real dainty touch. But her grip was as strong and steady as a quarterback's. And my skin tingled where she touched me.

"Now you're ready to add a spoonful of meat." Alex let go of my hand and motioned to a large pot sitting next to the dough.

"Mmmm. This smells good," I said, plopping a large mound of the mix onto my husk. "What's in it?"

"Well . . . pork roast and, uh, some other stuff."

"Like what?"

Alex hesitated.

"Meat from *la cabeza,*" Abuelita put in.

"*La* what?" I asked.

"The head of the pig," Gabriel said.

Clang! The spoon slipped from my grasp and bounced against the floor. Everyone immediately started laughing.

"It's the meat most tender and tasty," Blanca

explained. I didn't want any further explanation. My stomach was already beginning to capsize.

"You eat bacon, don't you?" Nina asked.

"Yeah, sure," I responded.

"Well, that's from the other end of the hog and people don't think that's gross. And do you know what goes into hot dogs?"

"*Bastante, Nina!* That's enough," Abuelita yelled. *"El hombre ya se ve enfermo."*

"Estoy solamente hablando, Mama. No importa."

"El no está aquí para hablar contigo. El está aquí para visitar con Alex."

I didn't know what they were saying, but I figured it was about me. Then when they mentioned Alex's name, I saw her blush a little.

"That's enough with the Spanish, guys," she announced. "You'll make Sean feel uncomfortable."

"That's okay. I don't mind," I said. "I took Spanish my freshman and sophomore years, but I'm still not too good at it."

"So practice with us," Gabriel suggested.

"Yes. Try it," urged everyone else.

"Nah, I'd just make a fool out of myself."

"Oh, come on," Alex said. "You can't learn if you don't try. Go ahead. I promise we won't laugh."

I glanced around at everyone's expectant faces and then settled on Alex's warm smile. "Well, okay, but . . . *estoy mucho embarazado.*"

Everyone cracked up. Gabriel fell out of his chair, giggling like a hyena.

"What? Was it that bad?"

"Uh, Sean," Alex said, trying to contain a laugh. "You just announced that you're very pregnant."

I wanted to dive into the dough and hide. "Oh. Well, I meant to say that I was embarrassed. Which I really am now."

"Don't feel bad." Alex patted my arm. "Your pronunciation was excellent."

"And I must say, you're hardly showing at all," Michael quipped, restarting Gabriel's laughing fit.

Alex's family was totally wacky but fun. Everyone kept bickering with everyone else—in a lighthearted way. Mrs. Lopez teased Alex about being too perfectionistic with her spreading. Alex got on Gabriel's case about being too sloppy. When Michael started talking to me about sports, Nina called him lazy and ordered him to chop more meat. So Michael said Nina was bossy and had to duck to avoid her rolling pin. It sort of reminded me of how my buddies and I picked on each other in the locker room. I felt right at home.

"What plans do you have for tonight, Sean?" Mrs. Lopez asked as she gathered the freshly rolled tamales into a pot.

"Nothing. Uncle Gary is on call, so we're not celebrating until tomorrow."

"Then you should join us for our dinner."

"Yeah! Come on, Sean," Gabriel urged.

Alex smiled. "It's only right you should be here since you helped out so much."

I was just sitting there, wondering what to say, when Michael walked over and pointed to the pile of tamales I'd assembled.

"Whoa, check those out!" he exclaimed. "They're as big as footballs."

Gabriel knelt in his chair to peer at my handiwork. "Look, Alex. They're twice as big as ours!"

He was right. While Alex and Gabriel had rolled their tamales into perfect sausage-size sticks, mine were as wide as a baseball bat.

"Oops. Sorry. I wondered why I was having a hard time keeping them closed. What am I doing wrong?"

Alex patted my arm again. "Don't worry. They look great, really. You might want to use a little less meat, though."

"Ay, your daddy would've loved those," Abuelita said, peering over Alex's shoulder. "He always said we didn't use enough *carne*."

"Sí." Blanca shook her head and smiled.

"What did he always say?" Nina asked. "From that really old commercial?"

"Where's the beef?" Michael exclaimed.

Everyone laughed for a couple of minutes, and then one by one they fell silent, their faces sad and thoughtful. Gabriel started pounding his spoon into the *masa*, his face all angry looking like it had been when I'd first met him.

"Come, Gabriel," Abuelita said, gently placing her hand on his arm. "*Ven conmigo*. Let's go to the store and buy some more pork roast."

"I'll come too, Mama," Michael said. "Let me drive."

Gabriel toweled off his hands and let himself be led out by his grandmother and uncle. Everyone else went back to their work, but the tempo was slower and sullen. A few minutes later Mrs. Lopez put down her spoon, excused herself, and hurried off to the back bedroom. Her two sisters followed.

Alex and I were left alone in the kitchen. Everything was silent except for the low rumble of a simmering pot. Alex sat motionless in her chair, staring down at a pile of empty corn husks. The worry lines had appeared on her forehead again, and her chin quivered slightly. It seemed like invisible strings were holding her up and that the slightest gust of air could send her tumbling.

"You okay?" I asked.

She blew a few strands of hair out of her face and looked over at me. "It's kind of sweltering in here, don't you think? What do you say we go on the balcony and get some fresh air?"

We stepped through a pair of French doors, and Alex gave a small sigh of relief.

"Are you okay?" I asked again.

"Yeah. It's just hard, you know. This is going to be the first Christmas since . . . since . . ." Her voice cracked slightly. She crossed her arms and grabbed her shoulders in a self-hug, as if she were cold. Tears began streaming down her cheeks.

Before I realized what I was doing, I reached

out and put my arms around her, drawing her toward me. The movement was automatic, like running a pass pattern. It just seemed natural.

"Shhh," I whispered into her ear. "It's all right."

I don't know how long I held her. She melted against me, letting me support her. I could feel the slippery smoothness of her hair under my fingers.

After a while Alex pulled back a little and raised her head. Our eyes locked, and we leaned into each other, letting our lips come together. I couldn't feel the floor beneath my feet or the cool sea breeze around me. There was only her. And me. For the first time in weeks I felt right. My head cleared, and all the stress I'd been carrying around with me disappeared.

Our mouths separated, and Alex smiled up at me. I smiled back, our noses barely touching.

But then all of a sudden the world started up again and that old, familiar doubt snuck back into its place inside me. *You've done it now, dude,* came a voice from within. *You've let yourself fall for a girl. She's got you now. She has the power to make a complete fool out of you—like Jo Beth did.*

I let go of Alex and stepped back, feeling angry and panicky and woozy all at the same time. It was true. I had gone and let a girl get inside my head again. How could I have been such a wimp?

Alex looked at me, confused. "Are you all right?" she asked.

"Yeah. I'm fine. I just need to go, that's all."

"Go?" she asked, sounding totally taken aback. "Go where?"

"I just remembered, I have to . . . uh . . . I have to make a long-distance phone call." I walked back toward the balcony door and turned the handle. "Sorry to run off, but it's important. My future depends on it."

I knew I wasn't making any sense, but I just had to get out of there. Alex's tormented look was weakening me like kryptonite zaps Superman. I needed to escape while I still had some power left.

"It was cool seeing you again," I said, not meeting her eyes. "Bye." I gave a quick wave and retreated, creeping through the living room and out the door before anyone could stop me.

And then I was free. But it wasn't like I had broken a tackle and wanted to dance into the end zone. It was more like I'd fumbled the ball.

"Foster, you are one stupid jerk," I mumbled, leaning against her front door.

Obviously as far as girls were concerned, I was still an easy target.

Ten

Devin

I WALKED BRISKLY along the beach sidewalk, dodging in-line skaters and people walking their dogs. The late morning sun was almost at full power, and I had to roll up my sleeves and undo a couple of buttons at the top of my shirt to keep from cracking a sweat. I couldn't believe it was Christmas Eve.

Back home my mother had probably already put the turkey into the oven and whacked my dad's hands several times as he tried to steal some lemon bars. Another half an hour and the doorbell would be ringing—the first in a steady procession of relatives coming to visit. By evening a dozen people would be holding hands around our dining-room table, saying grace. My mouth watered when I thought about Grandma's candied yams and Aunt Lorena's Mississippi mud pie.

Oh, well. At least I wasn't stuck at the kids' table, refereeing squabbles between Damon and our cousin Jesse.

For months I'd been anticipating Christmas, but being away from my family erased the holiday spirit. Today felt like any other day. The only thing I had to look forward to was meeting Halle for lunch. Thinking about her bright smile made me quicken my step a little. I couldn't wait to see her.

I just wished I could share my news about Halle with Sean. He'd have new respect for me. Although that morning he sure thought I was king of the dweebs.

I'd been racking my brain for a new cover story so I could get away and meet Halle. I couldn't say I was jogging since I didn't want to wear sweats or shorts to the restaurant, he knew I'd already finished my Christmas shopping (the day before I bought him a 49ers cap and wrapped it before he could peek), and I couldn't exactly tell him that the bat signal was shining overhead and local officials needed my extraordinary crime-solving abilities.

So, the best I could come up with was to tell Sean I needed to mail some souvenirs to my family. I could tell by his expression that he thought I was a card-carrying mama's boy, but at least he didn't harass me about it.

"Devin! Devin! Over here!"

Halle was standing at the end of the pier,

where we'd planned to meet. "Hey! Don't you look nice," she said, walking up to me.

"Thanks. So do you." She was wearing an itsy-bitsy cropped T-shirt, baggy jeans that were rolled up at the ends, and sandals that showed off her tattoo. Her long wavy hair was down, and her 49ers cap was at an angle.

"You ready to eat?" she asked, tugging at my arm. "Let's go. I'm starved."

We walked to the edge of the beach and crossed the street to find Kim's Korean Hut. The smells coming out of the entrance were intoxicating.

The restaurant was packed, but we managed to find a small table for two against the wall.

"Ah, Halle." A beautiful Korean woman in a yellow silk dress approached us. "Nice to see you. And you brought a friend today?"

"Hi, Eun Hee. This is Devin. It's his first time eating Korean."

"Ah. Very good. I'll bring you a combination platter so that you can try all the different Korean specialties at once. Would you like that?"

"Sure," I said. "Is that all right with you?" I asked Halle.

"Sounds great. I love everything they have here."

While we waited for the food, Halle chatted on about work, school, the watch she bought her father for Christmas, and her friends in San Francisco whom she usually visited over the holidays but couldn't this year since they were out of the country. She kept asking me things about myself, like whether I missed my folks, how my brother and I got along, that sort of thing. It was difficult keeping my responses brief. Halle was so good-natured and easy to talk to, I had to literally grit my teeth to keep from gushing out everything about myself.

"You know, I'm considering getting my nose pierced," Halle announced, wiggling her eyebrows irresistibly.

"No! Don't. Why would you do that?"

"Because I like the look," she replied with a shrug. "What? You don't like it?"

I shook my head. "I think you look perfect without it. I don't understand why people want to do things like that to themselves. Doesn't it hurt?"

"Who decreed that it's okay for women to get their earlobes pierced but not their noses? I mean, what's the difference? And I've got news for you. Women are used to enduring a little pain in order to look good. Getting your legs waxed? Hurts like hell. Plucking your eyebrows? Also stings. High heels? Don't even get me started. Not to mention orthodontics, reconstructive surgery, and cancer-causing suntans. So what's wrong with a little extra hole in my nose?"

I sat speechless as Halle paused to take a breath.

"You need to broaden your horizons a bit, Oklahoma boy," Halle teased, kicking me playfully under the table. "And by the way, thank you."

"For what?"

"For saying you think I'm perfect looking." She cocked her head demurely and smiled like the Cheshire cat.

She was right. A little bit of gold at the side of her nose probably wouldn't hurt her looks at all. Heck, she could have antennae sprouting from her forehead and still look gorgeous.

"Here's your special platter," Eun Hee said, setting down a gigantic tray full of rice, soup, and a dozen small bowls containing various meats and vegetables. "You have fun now. Enjoy."

"Thanks," Halle and I said at the same time.

I had no idea where to begin. Luckily Halle took it upon herself to instruct me on every single dish, even demonstrating how to eat it all. She tried to get me to use chopsticks, but I politely refused. I didn't want to look like a fool.

All of the food was delicious. There was an incredibly tender, zesty meat dish that Halle called *bulkogi,* more *chapchae,* and *kimchee,* an assortment of spicy fermented vegetables. Then I tried some sushi-looking rolls called *kimbap,* some seaweed stuff, and a wonton-type noodle called *yakimandu.*

"What's that?" I asked, pointing to a bowl of steaming liquid.

"That's *kimchee chighe.* It's sort of a hot vegetable soup. It's good, but be careful—they add lots of peppers to it."

"No problem," I said, slurping down a giant spoonful. "I like my food spicy. I put hot sauce on my tacos all the . . . *yaugh!*" A nuclear explosion suddenly went off in my mouth.

"Are you all right?" she asked, her eyes widening.

All I could do was sit there and go, "Ha! Ho! Hee!" like some sort of lunatic Santa Claus.

"God, I'm so sorry!" Halle exclaimed with a note of panic. "I should've stopped you. That stuff is tasty, but it burns if you're not used to it."

My mouth felt like it was in the throes of dental surgery, my esophagus had hardened into a car exhaust pipe, and it hurt to bring air into my body. *I'm done for,* I thought. *This must be a rare yet fatal allergic reaction to* kimchee chighe.

I couldn't talk, but I locked my watering eyes with Halle's and tried to send a telepathic farewell message: *You are the most beautiful and incredible girl I've ever met. Thank you for the wonderful yet brief time we had together. Please tell Sean I'm sorry. Tell my folks I love them and that Damon can have my computer. Goodbye, cruel world.*

I doubled over and put my forehead down on the table, coughing uncontrollably. Someone was doing tae kwon do on my backside. Then I realized it was Halle, patting me between the shoulder blades.

"Here," she said, sounding muffled and far off. "Eat some of this."

She handed me a couple of pieces of lettuce, which I slowly nibbled on. Eventually the pain subsided to a minor inferno, my sweating and coughing stopped, and I could breathe again.

I looked up and saw Halle standing over me like an angel of mercy.

"Thanks. I think I'm okay now," I said hoarsely.

"Oh, thank God! You had me worried sick. Your face turned all sorts of colors, like Christmas lights. I thought I was going to have to do mouth-to-mouth."

Hmmm. I briefly entertained the notion of faking another attack, but decided against it.

While Halle finished her meal, I chewed on the remainder of my rice. It seemed to help quench the smoldering embers in my mouth, and it wasn't like I'd be able to taste any new stuff anyway.

"And for dessert," Eun Hee announced, setting a small plastic tray on our table, "two fortune cookies. Thank you. Please come again."

"This is my favorite part," Halle said, handing me a cookie while breaking open the other one. "You first. What does it say?"

I cracked open the cookie shell. "It reads, 'A friend in need is a friend in deed.' Big wow. I've heard that before."

"Let me see." She reached over and snatched it from my hands. "That's a typo. Isn't it supposed to be one word, *indeed?*"

"I have no idea."

"Hmmm. And how does that apply to your life, I wonder?"

I thought about Sean sitting alone in the

condo drinking a Yoo-Hoo and watching Jerry Springer. For a nanosecond I felt really awful. *He* was a friend in need.

"Beats me. What does yours say?" I asked, changing the subject.

"It says, 'Love works in mysterious ways.' Don't I know it." She rolled her eyes.

"And how does that apply to your life, I wonder?"

"Beats me," she replied with a wry smile.

On the way out we argued over who would pay for the check. She insisted on paying for at least half if not all of it, but I finally won out. I handed the cashier my dad's credit card and told her that's how we do things on a date in Oklahoma.

"So chivalry is not dead," she commented.

"You got it. Hey, you should write fortune cookies."

As we were heading out the door we stopped to let a man come through. I took a passing glance at him, and then my head snapped back like a slingshot. The man was Bruce Willis. I'm talking King Macho, Tycoon of Testosterone himself, Mr. Bruce Willis. I blinked hard a couple of times, afraid that the *kimchee chighe* had made me hallucinate, but it was him, all right. He was dressed like a normal guy, in a white buttoned shirt and jeans, but there was no mistaking that stern brow or rugged jawline.

I froze with my hand on the door and stared at him. Halle, who hadn't seen him yet, practically walked right into me.

Bruce seemed to notice us. "Hey," he said, nodding at us politely. Then Eun Hee and a couple of waiters raced up to greet him.

"Come on," Halle said, pulling me out the door.

"Th-Th-That was . . . was . . ."

"Yeah, it was."

"But I thought you said no one famous ever comes here."

"Occasionally you'll find some of them out here slumming with the little people. Especially if a place has a cool reputation."

"He looked so . . . so . . . normal."

"What do you mean?" she asked, leading me across the street. "Did you expect him to have three arms?"

"I just didn't think he'd seem like such a regular guy." I was excited at having run into a giant celebrity, but I was also suddenly feeling somewhat unsettled. Maybe it didn't really matter what you looked like or what your personality was. Maybe standing out in a crowd was just something you were born with—like Bruce or Sean. I had a strange feeling that no matter how hard I tried, I'd never be seen as an ultracool dude like either of them.

"Stick of gum for your thoughts," she said, digging around in her pocket.

"Man, Bruce Willis," I muttered to myself. "I can't believe I saw Bruce Willis."

"Jeez, I never thought you'd be so starstruck. Here, I'll give you the ten-dollar tour. Want to take a picture of that railing? I think Johnny Depp once leaned against it. Oh, and see that stretch of beach? They shot a swimwear ad there a year ago. Want to touch the sand where Kathy Ireland perched her butt?"

"Come on. Lay off."

"Ooh, look! A bubble-gum wrapper. I bet it was dropped by Roseanne—*hey!*"

I reached up and plucked the 49ers cap off her head. "What have we here?" I teased. "Wait! I'm getting vibes from it. The person who owns this hat will be famous."

"Give it back!" she shouted, but she was smiling.

"No way. This will be very valuable one day. See, I'm picking up a signal from it. I see you five years from now. You represent a very famous restaurant chain. People are lining up to see you. You smile at them. A hat, just like this one, is on your head. Only it doesn't say 49ers. It says . . . hmmm, it's a little fuzzy . . . wait, here we go. It says Taco Bell."

"Oh, you are so dead."

She lunged forward with all her might, reaching up for the cap. Our feet got tangled up, and we crashed backward onto the beach. Halle continued to struggle and finally got a grip on the cap with both of her hands. But I wouldn't let go, and we ended up rolling around in the sand, wrestling like a couple of alley cats.

Finally, as I had her pinned down with both her wrists in one hand and her cap in the other, she laughed and said, "Okay, okay! Uncle! Whatever. I give! Can I please have my hat back?"

"Wait," I said slowly, letting go of her wrists and staring into her eyes. "I'm getting another psychic image from it. I can see the near future."

"What do you see?" she asked softly.

"I'll show you." I let my lips fall onto hers, and we kissed for a long, tender moment.

I practically danced all the way back to the condo.

By all outward appearances, I could have been diagnosed as having the flu: I was warm and weak, and my heart was racing faster than a 747. *What a kiss!* I had no idea a mere connection of mouths could cause such physical symptoms. I mean, kissing Tasha had always been nice, but this had charged every single one of my nerves, as if I'd stuck a fork in a toaster or something.

We had sat on the beach kissing and watching the waves roll in until I realized I needed to be getting back. As we said good-bye Halle asked me to join up with her at the coffee shop later on so I could meet her dad and go with her to a Christmas party. Then she gave me such an incredible kiss, I said yes without even letting my brain ponder it.

Oh, well, I'd think of some way to meet her. The day was full of miracles so far.

I decided not to wait for the elevator and hummed all the way up the stairs. When I emerged from the stairwell, I saw Sean standing in front of Gary's neighbor's door. It kind of caught me off guard, so I just stood there looking at him for a second.

Sean saw me and jumped. "What are you doing here? How long have you been standing there? Are you spying on me or something?"

"Er, uh, I just got here." I couldn't understand why he was so angry.

"I was returning a mop I borrowed the other day," Sean explained, nodding to the neighbor's door. "That's all!"

"Okay."

Sean stomped across the hall and opened Gary's door. "Well?" he asked. "Are you coming in or not?"

"I'm coming," I mumbled, then followed him inside.

A friend in need. The words of my fortune echoed in my head, and the rush of excitement I'd been experiencing drained out of me. No wonder Sean was barking at me. While I'd been sneaking around to visit a girl, he'd had nothing better to do than clean his uncle's condo.

Some lousy friend I was.

Eleven

Sean

MAN, SOME LOUSY friend I was. I talk my buddy into coming out to California and the dude was so bored, he had to run to the post office for entertainment. Meanwhile I was across the hall kissing a girl. A gorgeous girl. An incredible kisser. Someone who could melt me down to a puddle just by smiling at me.

Cool it, Foster! Unplug the teleplay!

I made up my mind to get a grip on things once and for all. So it took me a few days to get my head in the game. So what? I still had over a week left in California. Plenty of time to accomplish my mission. I owed it to myself. And I owed it to Devin.

All I had to do was totally avoid Alex—just go cold turkey. The girl had some sort of strange power over me, and any time spent with her seemed to stun my senses. I knew blowing her off would be a jerk thing to do, but better to do it that way than end up with my ego skewered again.

"Yo, Dev," I said, sitting on one of the dining-room chairs. "I know we haven't had much time to do guy stuff. Sorry, dude. I guess it took some time to get used to being on vacation."

"No sweat," he said. "I'm sorry too. It took me a while to . . . get the feel of the place. Plus we both had Christmas errands to run and all."

"Yeah." I felt a pang of guilt, remembering I still had to buy him a present. He'd already wrapped whatever it was he got for me, and I hadn't a clue what to get him. Only one more day left to shop. I reminded myself to ask Gary about it later—he always gave cool gifts.

Devin drummed his hands nervously on his knees. He looked totally lost in thought, which was happening to him a lot lately. I figured he was still all busted up about Tasha and Brad Culpepper. Maybe that was why he kept jogging all the time, to try to push those memories out of his mind—the way I kept pumping iron back home. Five days in California and he wasn't any better off than I was.

"I got it!" I announced. "What do you say we go out bowling tonight with Gary?"

"On Christmas Eve?"

"Why not? We aren't partying till tomorrow since Gary's so busy. I guess it's not how Martha

Stewart would do it, but who cares? It'll be good guy-bonding time. Anyway, what else are we gonna do? Go caroling?"

Actually, Devin and his family were probably the type of people who *did* go caroling on Christmas Eve. Dev opened his mouth as if to protest but closed it again. He zoned off for a minute, thinking it over, then nodded weakly. "Okay. Sure. Let's go."

"All right! We'll have a blast, man!" I was feeling better already.

"I just need to go out for a sec and . . . um . . . go to the store," he said, standing up. "I thought I'd pick up another case of sodas."

"Cool. We seem to be running low on food around here."

After Devin left, I got to thinking about Alex again. Even though I'd acted so weird to her earlier, she was probably still expecting me to join them for Christmas Eve dinner. I knew there was no way I could go. My decision to stop seeing her had to start immediately, and besides, I'd told Devin we'd hang out together. But I couldn't just not show up. That would be a low blow. And what if she came over here looking for me? How would I explain everything to everyone?

Nope, I had to go cancel our plans in person. One last time face-to-face.

I walked across the hall and knocked on the door, bracing myself for the offended look in

Alex's eyes when I told her. *Be cool, Foster. Don't let her get to you.*

Gabriel opened up the door. "Hi! I got back from the store and you were already gone, and you missed the first batch of tamales Abuela cooked, and some of yours were in there, only some of them were so big that they broke, but they tasted really good. Want some?"

I almost felt dizzy trying to follow his speech. "Uh, no. Thanks, dude. Is Alex around?"

"Yes, but she's in the shower. She said she smelled like the kitchen and wanted to be all clean and pretty for tonight. We're going to have lots of food. Uncle Michael brought his guitar, and he might sing for us too. He sings well, but he doesn't know any Hanson songs. Do you like—"

"Hey, listen, Gabriel. Um, I'm afraid I won't be able to make it tonight after all."

"Really? Why not?"

"Oh, something came up with my uncle. You know . . . family stuff."

I'd been somewhat prepared to handle a look of disappointment from Alex. I wasn't at all expecting to see Gabriel's face droop like a sad puppy dog's. It made me feel like the Grinch.

"I'm real sorry, buddy," I added, reaching over to mess up his hair.

"Can you come tomorrow? We always eat ham after opening presents. And there's a football game on too."

"I can't, sorry. But have fun. I hope you get

some killer loot from the man in the red suit."

"Thanks," he said quietly, looking down at the floor.

"Well, gotta go. Tell your family I said merry Christmas. I had a blast hanging with them today."

"Okay. Bye." He flashed me one last sad hound dog expression and then shut the door.

At least I didn't have to face Alex, I thought as I made my way back to Gary's. But letting Gabriel down made me feel just as awful.

Gary was standing at the dining room table, reading his mail, when I walked back into the apartment.

"Hey, Sean. I figured you weren't far since the door was unlocked. Where have you been? Where's Dev?"

"He went across the street to get some soda, and I was, um, taking a short walk to stretch my knee. But hey, I've got some good news, Scary."

"Really? What?"

"The three of us are going bowling tonight. A real guys' night out!"

"Tonight? Er, you sure you want to go on Christmas Eve?"

"Why not? Come on. I've been looking forward to us doing some guy stuff together since we got here. And we always have a great time at the bowling alley. Right?"

"Yeah. Yeah, we rule. It's just that . . . well . . . I have to make a call. I need to check on some stuff at the hotel before we go."

"All right, then! It's a plan! Oh, by the way, I need your advice on a Christmas gift for Devin."

"What did you have in mind?"

Just then the door opened and Devin walked in, carrying a case of Dr Pepper.

"Hey," he said.

"Hey." I turned back to Gary. "I'll tell you later on, okay?"

"Sure. I'll go make that call." Gary headed for his bedroom.

"Oh, and Gary?" I called after him. "Sorry about leaving the door unlocked."

"No sweat. I'm not worried. It just so happens, I have the coolest neighbors in the world."

That's a fact, I thought with a sigh.

Normally I really like bowling alleys. It's the only place where twelve groups of people can have their own dramatic sporting events side by side. Where you can eat a chili dog or play pinball between games. Where people are expected to wear nerdy shoes and ugly shirts and even the wimpiest-looking dude can be a sports star. This was guy-bonding paradise.

Unfortunately the night turned out sort of lame.

We found an alley that was open, but hardly anyone was there, which took away from the atmosphere of the place. At least we had our pick of lanes, shoes, and balls.

"Who wants to go first?" I asked, rolling

the ball in my hands. "Or shall we arm wrestle for top spot?"

"Nah, you go first. I don't mind," Devin said.

"Yeah, go ahead, Sean. I'll keep the score," Gary put in.

Both of them seemed kind of out of it, like they had a lot on their minds. Gary was probably wrapped up with work as usual. And Devin was probably a little homesick for Mommy and Daddy.

Actually, I was sort of preoccupied too. I couldn't shake the guilt I felt over flaking out on Alex and Gabriel. But I was still determined that we'd all have a blast.

As I prepared to take my shot I decided to put on a show to fire up the others. "First up, the Gipper. Notice his perfect form as he stalks fearlessly to the front of the lane, aims his shot, draws back his patented bionic arm, and . . . *bam!* The release! A little stiff because of his knee brace, but nevertheless eight pins are instantly vaporized. High fives all around. This will be the man to beat!"

Gary rolled his eyes and Devin shook his head as I swaggered back for my ball. A little more verbal prompting and I figured they'd get into the spirit.

"The Gipper gets ready for his next shot. The place is completely silent, watching in anticipation. . . ."

"I wouldn't say *completely* silent," Gary quipped.

"Again his form is pure art, his power unparalleled. He lines up his shot, releases, and . . . he scores! One more pin goes down for the count!"

Gary marked my score, slapped me on the back, and grabbed his ball.

"Next up," I continued with the play call, "Gary McGonagle, one of our senior players."

"Hey, watch it," he said. He threw back his arm and sent the ball skating along the lane like a cannonball on an air-hockey table.

"A strike! Not bad for an old geezer. Guess that Geritol must be working."

Gary socked my shoulder as he passed. Then Devin stood up to take his turn.

"Here we have the newest member of the group, a protégé of the Gipper, Mr. Devin Schaub. Notice Schaub's form closely resembles that of his teacher, although not quite as professional, and with the addition of a rude hand gesture toward the announcer. Stoically he lines up his shot, draws back, and releases. Whoa! A five-pin split! Not quite the results we were expecting."

"That's all right, Dev," Gary called out. "Don't listen to Cosell here. You the man!"

For a while I kept up my running commentary of the game, piling on all sorts of praise when I was up and making fun of their form when it was their turn. But when they didn't jump in, I started feeling stupid and stopped.

I told them a couple of dirty jokes, but their laughs seemed kind of fake. I raved about Gary's new truck and asked him about its horsepower and hauling capacity, but he didn't know much of the mechanics. I asked Devin how his running was going, but he wasn't real enthused about it. Every one of my efforts at turning the party around seemed to backfire on me.

Finally I turned to a guaranteed conversation starter: professional football.

"How about those 'Niners, man?" I said, elbowing Gary. "I told you San Francisco would be in the play-offs. They are Super Bowl bound."

"Yeah. Things look good."

"What do you think, Schaub?" I asked. "I mean, Green Bay looks good, but you gotta hand it to San Fran. When things go wrong, they tough it out and go for it, right? Like real men. You can always rely on the 49ers to come through."

"Can we please change the subject?" Devin snapped out of nowhere. He sat frowning, his jaw muscles quivering. It reminded me of the way he looked after catching Tasha with Brad.

"Hey, chill, dude. What'd I say?"

"Nothing. Just forget it. I'm going to get a hot dog." He stood up and stalked off toward the snack bar.

"Jeez, man," I said to Gary. "What do you think his problem is?"

"Beats me. Maybe he's a Cowboy fan." Gary rubbed his forehead as if he had a giant headache.

I couldn't believe the evening was turning out so bad. This was why we had come to

California. We were supposed to be feeling better about ourselves!

"Ah, who cares?" I grumbled. "Let Devin throw his baby tantrum. He's probably just homesick. Or he's upset that I'm beating him as usual—sore leg and all. You and I can still have fun, right, Scary?"

"You said it. It's a Kodak moment." He reached over and whacked me on the back, like he usually does when we're palling around. This time, though, it seemed different. I got the feeling he was hanging with me out of obligation or, worse yet, pity.

Gary and I finished the game one-on-one, but I ended up playing totally lousy. For some reason I felt like I was one of the pins out there at the end of the lane. First Jo Beth, then the Florida State scout, then Uncle Gary, then Devin and our pact. Lately I couldn't count on things to play out the way they were supposed to. I mean, Alex was the one good thing that had happened to me in a long time, but I couldn't let myself think about her. All I could do was stand there helplessly, waiting to get knocked over again and again and again. . . .

Twelve

Devin

THE NEXT MORNING I had to see Halle. The day before I'd called her from outside the nearby grocery store and canceled our plans. She wasn't at home, so I'd left a message—some lame story about Gary's car breaking down and stranding us in Los Angeles. I felt really guilty, so I probably didn't sound all that convincing.

I quickly dressed and left a note for Sean and Gary that I went jogging—which wasn't actually a lie since I ran the whole way to the coffee shop. Unfortunately when I arrived, there was a sign on the door saying they were closed for Christmas. All that way for nothing.

I headed back to the condo, thinking over everything that had happened recently. If only Sean would give up on the whole pact business, then things wouldn't be so complicated. I wouldn't have to lie anymore or sneak around, and I could introduce Halle to Sean—I knew he'd get a kick out of her. But he was completely fanatical about this no-women deal. If I confessed to him about Halle, he'd probably tell me to never see her again and make my stay a living hell. At least with the way things were, I could see her occasionally.

Suddenly up ahead I saw a familiar figure coming toward me. A girl with long legs was jogging along the beach wearing a 49ers cap. Halle.

"Hey! Halle! Over here!" I ran up and fell into step beside her. She saw me but gave no answer.

"I just came from the coffee shop. I was looking for you."

Again no response.

"I know you're upset with me about last night. I really did want to come, but . . . but the car just wouldn't start. It was really frustrating."

Halle exhaled loudly but kept her green eyes fixed straight ahead.

"I'm really sorry. I wanted to see you more than anything. I just couldn't. Will you give me another chance? Please?"

She suddenly stopped running, and I ended up several strides down the beach before I realized it and halted. By the time I got back to her, she was sitting cross-legged on the sand, staring out to sea.

"I looked great, you know," she said without looking at me. "I was wearing my black vintage dress and antique earrings. My hair had done just what I wanted it to do for a change. And I even dabbed a little perfume on my neck."

I felt a sinking sensation, as if the beach were made of quicksand.

"But the main reason I looked great was my mood," she continued. "I was so jazzed about seeing you. I hadn't felt that way in a long time."

Again I felt myself submerge, this time halfway to the earth's core.

"So I waited for you to call and waited and waited. Then finally I noticed the machine flashing and heard the messages. 'Sorry,' you said. 'The car broke down.'" She looked directly into my eyes. "Where exactly were you stranded in LA?"

My mind strained to find an answer before I blew my cover. "The doctor's office. Dr. Culpepper's. My buddy Sean is still sick, and we took him in."

"Mmmm," she murmured, nodding. Once again I felt as if she were scrutinizing everything about me. "What does he have anyway? Some sort of bug?" she asked.

"Er, yeah. A horrible virus. Probably caught it flying over. You know how bad that airplane air is. The doctor told him to just take it easy." I knew she was testing me, so I met her gaze and forced myself to stay calm and collected.

Be Sean, I told myself.

While her emerald eyes penetrated mine, I reached over and gently brushed a lock of hair out of her face. "I bet you looked fantastic in your black dress," I said, smiling. "I'm really sorry I missed it. And I'm sorry I let you down."

Halle's shoulders relaxed, and her eyes ceased their laserlike probing of my mind. "No, I'm sorry," she said. "When you canceled on me, I automatically assumed you were lying. Unfortunately after Wade made a fool out of me, I've been having a hard time trusting people. Not that I was ever that good at it."

I didn't know what to say. A whole slew of emotions paraded through me. Relief. Guilt. Sympathy. Frustration. She looked at me with a sweet, bashful smile, and my heart swelled like a balloon. I leaned over, lifted the brim of her cap, and kissed her on the forehead. Then she put her hands on the sides of my face and gently pulled my lips to her level.

I had no idea how Sean could manage to stay cool while kissing a woman. I felt like my protective coating of mystery was immediately burned off whenever Halle's lips met mine. My brain stopped functioning, and I'm sure I had a really dopey smile on my face.

"I know a way you can make up for canceling on me last night," she said. "Promise me you'll take me out on a date. A real evening out. I'm tired of meeting for jogs and quick lunches. Tonight my dad and I have some Christmas stuff planned, but what do you say we do something tomorrow night?"

"Sure!" You have to remember that my mind was completely shut down at this point. The logical part of me that could have pointed out the impossibility of an evening away from Sean was being bound and gagged by my sappy, love-struck side.

"Great!" she said. "Why don't you meet me at Blinkers around six? I get off at five—that'll give me an hour to get all dolled up for you. Is it a date?"

"It's a date."

A date? I thought as I sat on the couch back at the condo. By now my common sense had freed itself from its emotional cocoon and was yelling at me. *What the heck were you doing making a date?*

Okay, think, Devin. You can handle this. Think of a plan.

Luckily Gary was out picking up some stuff for dinner and Sean was in the bedroom wrapping gifts, so I was able to concentrate without interruption. There had to be some way I could get away for a few hours the next evening.

Church! That was it! I could tell Sean that it was a strict family tradition that I attend church the night after Christmas. That way I could dress nice without suspicion and would be guaranteed to be able to go alone since Sean never went in for things like that. It was brilliant! So what if Sean thought I was as square as a Rubik's Cube? I'd get to see Halle.

After I'd worked out the minor details, I felt

much better. In fact, I was suddenly full of Christmas spirit, with visions of Halle dancing in my head.

"Okay, don't laugh," Sean said as he emerged from Gary's bedroom. "I'm no good at this wrapping stuff. So don't make fun, or you won't get to open it."

On the bar he set down a tattered-looking present. It was sort of odd shaped and rumpled looking.

"It looks fine," I said, smiling. "Don't sweat it."

I got out Sean's present and set it on the bar too. Then Gary walked in with a huge cardboard box.

"Hot stuff here," said Gary, waggling his eyebrows.

As Sean and I watched in awe Gary began to pull all sorts of succulent-looking gourmet foods from the box. There was a platter of duck orange, a big bowl of rice pilaf, some steamed asparagus, Caesar salad, and for dessert a lemon meringue pie. Now *this* was a Christmas dinner. Looked like my worries of canned chili and Twinkies were over.

"Whoa, Scary. Where'd you get all the fancy food?" Sean asked.

"From François, the chef at the hotel. I had him make a special meal for us."

"Wow. Thanks," Sean gushed.

"Yeah, thanks, Gary," I chimed in. "It looks incredible."

It was. Gary found a radio station that was playing Christmas music, and we all sat down at the table for our feast. He even found a huge candle someplace and lit it. Everything was fantastic. For close to an hour we ate and drank soda and laughed at the stories Gary told us about the unusual people who stayed at the hotel. Even though it wasn't exactly like the homey festivities at my house, I still felt more relaxed than I had in a week.

"Okay," Gary announced, pushing his chair back from the table. "Who wants to open presents?"

We gathered in the living room. Sean plopped onto the couch next to Gary, and I settled my overstuffed midsection into the recliner. Then Gary handed me a long, flat box.

"Aw, Gary. You shouldn't have bought me anything. I feel bad now that I didn't get you a present."

"Don't sweat it, Devin. I didn't expect anything—I mean, you've only known me a week. I just saw this in the hotel gift shop and thought you might like it."

I opened the box and pulled out a large gray sweatshirt with California, USA, lettered across the front.

"Cool! This is great. Thanks a lot."

"Sure."

Next Sean opened my gift to him.

"All right! The 'Niners!" he exclaimed, placing the hat on his head. "Thanks, buddy."

"You're welcome. And by the way, I do think they'll stomp Green Bay to get into the Super Bowl. Sorry about wigging out on you last night. I was just tired."

"It's forgotten, dude. No sweat." He fiddled with the brim of his cap and turned to Gary. "Uh, Uncle Scary. You know I chipped in on the suit Mom sent you a couple of weeks ago. I didn't really bring anything else."

"I know, and I loved it. Although I have to get the jacket altered since I seem to have, uh, stretched in the middle a bit." He rubbed his stomach and smiled sheepishly. "There's too much apologizing going on here. I don't care about getting things. I mean, look around. I don't need much. But I do want you to have this."

Gary pulled an envelope from his shirt pocket and handed it to Sean.

"A check for a thousand bucks?" Sean asked after he'd ripped it open. His mouth gaped open and his eyebrows lifted so high, I thought his new cap would pop off his head.

"For college," Gary explained. "I know you'll need books and supplies, not to mention plenty of Pop-Tarts. This will help."

"But . . . but . . . Scary. This is too much money. I can't take all this."

"Sure, you can." Gary reached over and gave Sean a big monster hug. "I'm proud of you, man."

They hugged for a while, pounding each other on the back like they were putting out fires. I could see the emotion in Sean's face, and for a brief instant I wondered if he might cry. But as usual he stayed cool. Only a slight waver in his voice as he whispered, "Thanks, dude," gave him away.

I guess it's true what people say about Christmas. It didn't seem to matter that there wasn't an ornately decorated tree in Gary's condo or a jar full of Grandma's sugar cookies on the kitchen counter. It was all about giving and showing people how much they mean to you. Watching Sean and Gary, I found myself feeling really sentimental.

"Devin, my man. This is for you." Sean handed me the package he'd brought out earlier.

I tore open the paper, lifted the lid of an old shoe box, and looked inside. There lay two rectangular pieces of paper. I picked them up.

"Tickets to see the Roman Candles?" They were one of my favorite bands. When they came through Tulsa over the summer, I couldn't go. Sean knew how disappointed I'd been.

"Yeah, can you believe it? They're playing at this club not too far from Gary's hotel," he explained excitedly. "Gary was able to scam some tickets even though the show's been sold out for weeks."

"Wow! Thanks, guys!" My holiday was complete. I had good food, good buddies, a date with a goddess the next evening, and now tickets to see one of the coolest bands around. Deck the halls. Joy to the world.

"We are going to have a blast tomorrow night!" Sean went on.

My heart stopped. "Tomorrow night?"

"Yeah. That's when the concert is," Sean

replied. "Man, it's gonna jam! Everyone back home will be so jealous."

My holiday joy squirted out of me like ketchup from a squeeze bottle. I looked at the tickets in my hands. Sure enough, the fine print read December 26, 8:00 P.M.

"I'm so glad it worked out," Gary said. "For a while I didn't think I'd be able to get you guys seats, but then a connection of mine came through. You are two very lucky dudes."

Yeah, I thought glumly. *Very lucky.*

Thirteen

Sean

YOU KNOW HOW sometimes a song or jingle gets stuck in your head? That's how it was with me and thoughts of Alex. No matter how hard I tried, I couldn't get her out of my mind. Little things I would see or hear could trigger an image of her as fast as hitting a remote control: the sound of someone in the hallway outside the condo. The smell of seasonings in the rice. A commercial for Disneyland showing a bunch of people having a blast on the roller coaster.

And then sometimes nothing specific would remind me of her, but a little mental movie would start to roll on its own. Usually I'd picture Alex and me on her balcony—her beautiful, hypnotic eyes, the smoothness of her arms, her soft lips touching mine. Sometimes I would zone out for minutes at a time, reliving it all. And the worst part was, the daydreams seemed to be getting *more* frequent instead of less.

I canceled my Christmas Eve plans with her, then avoided her entirely Christmas Day. Yet on the morning after Christmas, I sat on the couch replaying reel after reel of Alex scenes, wondering if it would ever stop. It was like going through some sort of weird withdrawal.

I had to do something to clear my mind and occupy my time; otherwise I'd go stark raving mad.

But what could I do? Like an inmate searching for a means of escape, I frantically looked around the room. The place was a mess. Tiny shards of wrapping paper and pie crumbs were all over the floor, towers of dirty dishes loomed on the kitchen counter, and the entire condo smelled like that orange duck stuff we'd eaten the night before. I decided I'd clean up a bit.

I shouldn't have been surprised that Gary didn't have a vacuum cleaner. I already knew he didn't have a mop or a broom. Plus there still wasn't any dishwasher detergent, and I'd used up the last of the dishwashing liquid when I'd caused the soap bubble mess.

Soap bubbles . . . slippery floor . . . Alex falling into my arms. . . .

Another motion picture started up in my mind.

Auugh! Snap out of it, Foster!

I couldn't wait until the concert later that

evening. That would definitely take my mind off Alex.

"Why won't they let us in? They said eight o'clock!" I tapped my right foot impatiently as we stood outside the club.

Devin shrugged. "That guy said something about a bomb threat they had to check out. But maybe it's just a gimmick the band thought up."

There were tons of people waiting in line outside Club Haus to see the Roman Candles. In front of us stood four girls in miniskirts who kept swooning over the band.

"Oh, my God! I can't wait to see them in person! I want to stand right in front of Carl Cutter. I want his sweat to fall on me!" She screeched and wiggled her shoulders excitedly.

All four let out high-pitched squeals and hopped up and down like rabbits. Devin and I looked at each other and rolled our eyes. Then someone tapped me on the shoulder from behind. I turned around and saw a woman in a blue dress holding a microphone. In back of her stood a dude with a video camera pointed at us.

"Excuse me, sir. I understand they're having to delay the show while they check out a bomb threat in the building. How do you feel about that?" asked the woman, holding the mike out toward me.

Normally I'd be stoked about being on a TV news spot, even ham it up for the viewers at home. But being out among lots of girls was throwing off my cool attitude. "Uh, well, I sure hope those dudes check the place out well. Especially under *my* seat."

She gave me a phony smile and then turned to Devin. "What about you, sir? Do you feel your safety might be compromised tonight?"

"No, not really," he said in his honor-roll-student voice. "I mean, I knew I'd have a *blast* tonight. But I wasn't expecting this."

By now the Roman Candles cheerleaders in front of us were crowding around me and Devin, trying to get on camera.

"So I take it you're big fans?" the lady asked me.

"Yeah—they rock," I said.

Again she moved the mike toward Devin. "They're excellent," he told her, trying for extra credit. "I think their lyrics really speak for teenage America."

Meanwhile the giggly girls kept falling all over us, yelling, "Candles! Candles! Whoo-oo!"

Luckily at that point the front doors opened and everyone on the street started racing into the place. I couldn't move too fast because of my knee, and Devin, being such a good guy, kept pace with me. Eventually we got in.

The place looked like a giant cellar. The stage stood at one end, and bleachers ran along the sides and back. In the middle was a big concrete floor for dancing or moshing. Most of the crazed fans who ran into the place ahead of us were already packing the pit like matchsticks. Dev and I, however, headed for the bleachers. We were big fans, but I still had a bum knee and he wasn't the moshing type.

We got great seats in the middle section, close enough to see the band but high enough to see over the crowd. I was feeling totally stoked.

"It's starting!" Devin shouted.

Sure enough, the lights went dim, the crowd whooped, and a short man with a thick mustache walked onstage. "Sorry about the delay. We thank you for your patience. Now, we at Club Haus are pleased to present the Roman Ca—"

Girlish screams drowned out the rest of his sentence. The stage lights went out, and when they snapped back on, the band had "magically" appeared. Immediately they launched into a song, my favorite, a tune called "Happy Daze."

"Yeah!" I hollered, waving my fist in the air. It was going to be my night, for sure.

Already I felt better. Devin and I tapped our feet to the music and drummed our hands on the bleacher seats as Pablo Mendez, the lead singer, and Carl Cutter, the bass player, harmonized about a girl with angel eyes.

Suddenly, as I listened to the song, I stopped bopping my head. I'd never paid much attention to the lyrics before. But all of a sudden it seemed like the song was talking to me.

"A sad-eyed beauty who puts me in a trance . . . ," the chorus began.

I tried to stop listening to the words and just concentrate on the killer bass riff instead. *It's just one tune,* I thought. *It's not like all their songs are about schmaltzy stuff.*

Boy, was I wrong. Their next piece was a slow ballad called "I Dry Your Tears." Pablo crooned into the microphone as if he were half bawling. Couples all around us started to put their arms around each other and sway back and forth. It was all I could do not to puke.

Devin didn't seem to notice the funk I was suddenly in. He just kept watching the band and tapping his feet to the slow rhythm.

Meanwhile I gritted my teeth and got through the song. Unfortunately the next few tunes, even though they were faster, were also about meeting a girl or kissing a girl or taking a long drive in a '57 Chevy to get over a girl. I'd never realized how limited their material was. Everything reminded me of Alex or Jo Beth or people's stupid obsession with romance.

What was this? A conspiracy? I was being betrayed by one of my favorite bands and surrounded by love-crazed losers. What made me think a concert would do me good?

An hour went by. I knew I couldn't stand it much longer. One more reference to women and I was ready to rush the stage like all those screeching girls the stagehands were holding back. Only instead of trying for a lock of hair, I wanted to choke all the sappy sentiment out of Pablo's vocal cords.

"Please be the last song. Please be the last song," I muttered under my breath.

"You guys have been great," Carl Cutter said over the audience's cheers. "We have time for one more song."

Thank God! Not only were they ending their show, but the last tune turned out to be not at all mushy. It was a song called "Half Gods," and even though I couldn't understand all the lyrics, it seemed to be more about religion than anything.

I got back into the spirit. Dev and I cheered and whistled and bounced in our seats. Afterward we hollered along with everyone else to get the band back onstage for an encore. And I was relieved that they chose to play a pumped-up version of a Beach Boys surfing song.

"Thanks a lot for the tickets," Devin said later as we waited on the curb for Uncle Gary to pick us up. "It was a killer show."

"Yeah, it was cool."

"Those guys really rock," he went on, shaking his head in awe. "I mean, I knew they were good, but they blew me away tonight. What's your favorite song of theirs?" he asked.

"Oh, I don't know. Probably 'Half Gods.'"

"Really? Me too! I saw Carl Cutter talking about it on MTV. It's based on a Ralph Waldo Emerson poem. He said it was about how when you let go of someone who wasn't meant to be, you make room for someone who is.

Like the lyrics say, 'When the half gods go, the gods arrive.' Kinda cool, huh?"

"Yeah," I responded, trying to hide my frustration.

Great, I thought miserably. *From now on, no more songs with lyrics. I'll listen to Beethoven and Yanni for the rest of my life.*

Fourteen

Devin

THE MORNING AFTER the concert I overslept. By the time Gary had picked us up the night before and we'd driven back to Newport Beach, it had been pretty late. Then I couldn't get to sleep.

I was feeling guilty about enjoying the show so much. Earlier that day I'd called Halle from the pay phone and canceled our date. She seemed really perturbed until I told her that Sean had taken a turn for the worse. I said that I was really worried about him (which wasn't a total lie) and that I promised to take her out another evening—as soon as he felt better. She immediately softened up and told me she understood. Then we agreed to meet the next morning for a jog, and the conversation ended pleasantly. But later that night, as I tossed and turned on the futon, I felt like a total jerk for having manipulated her.

And I must have been totally out of it because I set my watch alarm for 7 P.M. instead of A.M. At 7:34 I awoke to the sound of Sean humming a Roman Candles song in the shower.

"Oh, no!" I cried, hurriedly throwing on my clothes and then running out the door.

"Please be there, please be there, please be there, please be there," I continued chanting as I raced down the stairs and out onto the beach. But with the exception of a couple of seagulls squawking overhead, the area was vacant. "Aw, no!"

How could I explain this to Halle? As I pondered my dilemma I started running full throttle toward the pier—partly out of desperation and partly out of habit. I was just about to stop and admit failure when I spotted her. She was about a football field ahead of me, but there was no mistaking the cap, legs, and perfect stride. Somehow I activated a turbo boost that sped me up and narrowed the gap between us.

"Halle!" I called as I came closer to her. "Hey, Halle!"

She must have been wearing her CD Walkman because she didn't turn around. In fact, it almost seemed like she was speeding up. Again I shifted into high gear.

"Halle! Halle, it's me! Haaaalleeee!"

She didn't stop. But I was finally close enough to see her clearly, and I noticed she didn't have her earplugs in. She could hear me all right—she just didn't want to talk to me. She thought I'd stood her up!

Halle was doing everything she could to shake me. She left the beach and started jogging along the sidewalk, weaving in and out among the pedestrians. I tripped over a couple of dog leashes and had to vault over a double stroller, but luckily I managed to stay with her.

"Halle, please! Let me explain!"

I guess Halle decided it was time for some serious evasive maneuvers because she veered off the sidewalk and started running through a nearby parking lot. It was like chasing a frightened cheetah. Not only was Halle fast, she could wend her way around cars and fire hydrants like a leaf in the wind.

"Halle! I'm sorry! Let me talk to you!"

We probably looked kind of silly, and I noticed a couple of people cast uneasy stares in my direction. I briefly visualized myself being led away by two burly street cops for jaywalking, harassment, disturbing the peace, and showing up twenty minutes late for a date.

"Wait! Just hear me out!"

A piece of sharp metal sticking out from the bumper of a truck scraped my thigh. My legs felt like cement posts, and my stomach was beginning to cramp up. But I forced myself to keep following her retreating ponytail.

"Please, Halle!" My throat was so raw from

breathing hard that I barely had a voice anymore.

Halle exited the parking lot, ran through the gates of an apartment complex, and finally came to a stop beside a swimming pool. Slowly and calmly, she turned to face me as I approached. Her face was bright red.

"Thank God!" I exclaimed, trudging toward her. "I am *so* sorry. I set my watch wrong and overslept. I hope you weren't waiting long."

"No. Not long at all," she replied, lifting her chin defiantly.

"Oh, I'm so glad. I can't believe I did that. I've had that watch for years, and I've never messed it up. What a dork, huh? Heh, heh, heh." I laughed nervously as I met her stony gaze.

"Rough night?" she asked.

"Yeah. Er, real rough. Sean had a really high fever and—"

"Big fat liar!" Halle shouted. Before I could react, she lunged toward me and pushed me headlong into the pool. Cold water hit me like a wall of bricks, shocking my senses and filling my still-open mouth.

When I resurfaced, Halle was crouched by the side of the pool, rage flashing in her eyes like nuclear radiation.

"After you called off our date last night, I had nothing better to do than break open a bag of Funyuns and watch *Letterman.* When I turned on the TV, the evening news was just ending, and what do I see but you standing in line for the

Roman Candles, surrounded by several perky, and very *healthy looking,* friends."

Her words hit me harder than the icy water. "Oh, no. Halle, I'm sorry. Everything has been such a mess. You see, my friend wanted us to—"

"Don't! Don't you dare try to lie your way out of this! I can't ever believe another word you say!"

"I—I know. I don't blame you," I gurgled through heavily chlorinated water. "I wanted to tell you the truth, but—"

"Save it for the jury. I know your type." Halle stood up and clenched her fists. "You know, you had me so fooled. I thought you were a really nice guy. You seemed like someone who would catch a spider and set it outside rather than flatten it with your shoe. I . . . I trusted you!"

I reached over, grabbed the side of the pool, and started to pull myself out, but Halle stomped down on my fingers.

"Yow!" I exclaimed, falling back into the water.

"I should have known all along," she continued screaming at me. "You seem all sweet and trustworthy, but you're just like Wade. Sick friend. Broken phone lines. Car trouble. Yeah, right! Just how many other girls have you been winning over with that southern charm, huh? No wonder you could only meet me for jogs. I was your morning date! Your lunch, dinner, and movie slots were already filled!"

"No! No, I didn't—"

Halle grabbed a small potted plant off a

nearby ledge and threw it into the pool, narrowly missing my head.

"I don't ever want to see you again!" she hissed. Then she turned and ran off, disappearing into the sunshine.

A few people stood watching nearby, as if we'd been putting on a play just for their enjoyment. I climbed out of the pool and squeezed the water from my clothes, feeling completely humiliated. Not because strangers had seen us fight, but because of the harsh words Halle had pelted me with.

She actually thinks I've been cheating on her. Me? *Cheating on* her?

A horrible wave of nausea washed over me. All this time I'd wanted to be mysterious and cool. Instead I turned out behaving like Brad Culpepper!

Face it, I thought as I headed back to the condo, my shoes squishing with every step. *You aren't cool. You never will be. Halle deserves someone better.*

Fifteen

Sean

THE MORNING AFTER the Roman Candles show, I got up early. I couldn't sleep because of all the dippy love songs ringing in my head.

Gary was sleeping late, and the Eagle Scout was gone by the time I got out of the shower—probably out running as usual. Just great. Being alone in the condo with nothing to do gave my brain free license to daydream. I couldn't take much more of it.

A knock sounded. Yes! A diversion! I opened the door to find Gabriel standing in the hallway.

"Hi! You wanna come over and play with my new Sega? I got it for Christmas. And I got some cool discs too. I even got a football game. I wanted the one where they show the replay from all over, but instead

I got the one with zoom-in, super-slo-mo replay. It's cool, though. Ambulances come on whenever some-one gets hurt. You wanna see?"

"I'd love to, but . . . I'm going somewhere with my uncle."

He paused for a second and cocked his head. "Who's that I hear snoring in the background? Is that Mr. McGonagle?"

"Er, yeah. But he should be awake soon."

"Aw, please! We won't play long, I promise. No one ever wants to play it with me, and I'm tired of doing it by myself. I always lose." He looked so sad, I could hardly handle it. His toes turned inward, his shoulders drooped, and his forehead was all rippled, just the way Alex's gets.

"What about your sister? Can't she play with you?"

"Nah, she's sorry. She never knows where the ball goes. Anyway, she's not home. She went out to do laundry. I was supposed to ask you guys if I needed help."

"I think she meant if you had an emer-gency or something."

"Yeah, well . . ." He looked down at the floor and shuffled his feet back and forth. "I'm tired of being all by myself."

I felt like I'd been kicked in the intestines. How could I let him down? Besides, with Alex gone, I didn't have to worry about seeing her.

"All right. I'll come over. But I can only play a couple of games, okay?"

We walked over to his place and sat in front of the TV set in the living room. Gabriel was really proud of his new system. In a serious, expert-sounding voice he described everything he was doing in order to start up the game. I nodded along as if I'd never seen anything like it in my life. Then as we played I purposefully chose some bad plays for my own team and fumbled with the joystick enough to make sure he beat me.

"All right! I won!" he whooped as the timer ran out.

"Yeah, you totally stomped me."

"Don't feel bad," he said consolingly. "You tried really hard."

Just then Alex came through the front door, carrying a big basket of laundry. She looked so shocked to see me, you'd have thought I'd jumped out at her wearing a funny hat and yelling, "Surprise!" Part of me was glad to see her. The other part of me felt like I'd been busted doing something illegal.

"Hey," I said. "How's it going?"

"Fine," she said, smiling at me. Only it wasn't an actual, cheerful-looking grin—it looked forced and phony. "Gabriel, I want you to take this basket into your room and fold and put away your clothes."

"Aw, man! But Sean and I were gonna play another game! I'm winning!"

"Then you better do it now. You don't want to get pulled out in the middle of a game."

"Jeez! You always have to interrupt me when I'm having fun," Gabriel mumbled as he grabbed the basket of laundry and walked off.

Alex waited until she heard Gabriel's door close, then she turned toward me.

"I'm surprised to see you here," she said.

"Really? Why?"

"Come on, Sean. You left so suddenly that day we were on the balcony . . ." She paused for a couple of seconds, her eyes darting around the room. ". . . *talking.* Then you suddenly cancel our plans, and I don't hear from you for two days. It doesn't take a Nobel-prize-winning physicist to figure out why."

I gulped. Did she know the hold she had over me? Was she planning on infiltrating my last line of defenses and going in for the kill? *Play it cool, Foster,* I told myself. "Yeah, well, I'm sorry about all that. I just got busy with, uh, Christmas stuff and—"

"Oh, stop! You know, it's one thing to play games with me. I can handle it. I feel stupid for having fallen for your slick maneuvers, but I'll get over it." Her eyes started to mist up, and her voice grew shaky. "Gabriel, on the other hand, can't."

"What are you talking about?"

"You've lifted his spirits. He hasn't been this happy in a long time. He really likes you, and all you're doing is goofing around—you think hanging out here is just a nice little diversion for you."

"No! I just—"

"His heart was broken when our father died, and you're the first person he's been able to care about since." By now her bottom lip was trembling and her voice sounded high and raspy, as if her throat were closing up. "But if all you're going to do is play around for a week or so, then leave and never call again, you might as well stop now. I don't think we—I mean *he*—could handle being hurt by you."

"Are you telling me to get lost?" I couldn't believe it. She was tossing me out like a sack of trash. It was happening to me again!

"Better to stop things now than later," she muttered, angrily narrowing her eyes at me. "Don't come over here anymore, Sean."

"But—but you've got it all wrong," I began desperately. For days I'd been trying to crase her face from my mind. Now, all of a sudden, the thought of never seeing her again made me feel all panicky.

"I think you should leave," she said firmly. Before I could say anything more, she took off, disappearing down the hall toward the bedrooms.

And I went back to Gary's condo, feeling defeated—and not just at Sega football.

How could she do this to me—blow me off just because I cut out on her for a couple of days? I mean, it wasn't like we were in love or anything, right?

A pain swelled through my gut. Somehow I

felt even worse than I had after Jo Beth had dumped me. A lot worse. In fact, my eyes and nose stung a little and my throat felt all tight . . . no way was I going to cry, though. Instead I tried to focus on my anger.

Alex thought she had me all figured out. She thought I wasn't good enough for her or Gabriel, so she kicked me out— just like that. No warning. No second chances. And no listening to my explanations.

That's what you get for letting yourself get wrapped up with a girl again. You should've known better.

I wondered if pounding on something would make me feel better, like when I'd gone ballistic on that papier-mâché horse. I knew I had to do something—and soon. I couldn't let Devin or Gary see me all busted up like this.

The phone rang, making me jump. I took a deep breath and picked up. "Hello?"

"Uh, hi? Is Gary there?" a female voice asked.

"He's still asleep. Who's this?"

"Julie. I'm his—"

"Yeah, I know who you are," I snapped. *The cleaning lady who never cleans,* I thought. "Gary's told me all about you. Well, listen. I don't think you should be calling or coming by anymore. Gary isn't happy with the way things are working out, and he's looking for someone else."

"What?" she shrieked. "Who is this?"

"I'm his nephew. I'm staying in this pigsty for a couple of weeks. Not that it's any of your business."

"Put Gary on now! I want to talk to him!" she ordered.

"Look, trust me. It's better you hear it from me than him. From now on you won't be needed. Have a nice day."

I hung up the phone before she could screech any further protests in my ear. What an attitude! She does shoddy work and then has the nerve to act surprised when she's fired.

I know it sounds totally awful, but it had felt good to lash out at someone. Maybe I wouldn't need to punch something after all.

"Hey," Gary said, coming out of his bedroom. He stretched his arms and yawned. "Was that the phone I heard?"

"Yeah. It was just that cleaning lady Julie."

His sleepy eyes suddenly popped wide open. "Yeah? What did she say?"

"Not much. I did most of the talking, actually. I told her you thought she was lame and you were looking to replace her. And I said she shouldn't come by anymore."

"You what?"

"Yeah. I figured I'd save you the trouble of having to get rid of her. She sure wasn't happy about it, though. Man, what a spaz!"

Gary ran back into his room, reemerging with his pants and shoes. "Um, there's some stuff I need to do this morning," he said as he quickly threw on his clothes. "You guys go have fun without me."

"But I thought this was your day off. Is everything all right? You seem really stressed."

"Uh, yeah. I'm fine. I just have to . . ." He hopped around while hurriedly slipping on his shoes. "Uh . . . look into something. Something I've been neglecting for a while. You know how crazy things can get." Gary opened the door and ran out. "Later!" he called over his shoulder.

"Later," I responded, staring stupidly at the Lopezes' front door across the hall. Then I slowly shut Gary's door, gradually cutting off the view.

Yeah, Gary, I thought. *I know how crazy things can get.*

Sixteen

Devin

"YOU'VE RUINED MY life! Ruined it!" the woman on the TV screen screamed. "You and your horrible, wretched lies! I wish I'd never met you!"

"What's her beef?" Sean asked.

"I dunno. She just found out that the guy she loves is actually his evil twin or something. He was pretending to be her boyfriend in order to marry her, kill her off, and then inherit her wealth."

"Uh-huh. So where's the other dude? The real one?"

"Beats me. Probably chained in the attic."

"Mmmm." He nodded meditatively. "Hey, want some more Doritos?" he asked, handing me the bag.

"Thanks."

Sean and I had nothing better to do than sit

around and watch soap operas. Neither of us had any energy—he seemed to be in as foul a mood as I was. I don't know what Sean was mulling over, but I couldn't stop thinking about the awful fight Halle and I had the day before.

"I loved you," the woman continued, "and all you did was lie to me! How could you deceive me like that?"

She could have been screaming at me. Ever since I'd arrived in California, I'd done nothing but lie to everyone. I lied about where I was going, what I was doing, how I was feeling, and why I was acting a certain way. In fact, just the day before, when I came back to the condo sopping wet from getting pushed in the pool, I'd told Sean a long, drawn-out lie that could be worthy of a Pulitzer.

I stammered that after I'd gone for a hard run, I'd decided to stretch out on the beach and rest. Then I fell asleep, and the next thing I knew the tide must have come in because water came splashing up all over me. Sean stared at me and shook his head, no doubt thinking that I'd left 80 percent of my gray matter back in Saddle Pass. But at least he didn't rib me about it. He seemed too wrapped up in his own thoughts.

"Aw, gross!" Sean exclaimed, gesturing to the TV. "More of this puke."

There was a different woman and man on the screen, locked in a romantic embrace.

"Oh, Chet! You're my whole life," murmured the actress. "I'll love you forever!"

"Yeah, right," Sean groaned. "Till someone better comes along. What a load of garbage!"

I couldn't bear to watch it myself. The woman's smoldering green eyes reminded me of Halle. As the people on-screen began kissing passionately, I tried to concentrate on the recommended daily allowance of fiber that Doritos provide.

"These shows are a total crock!" Sean went on. "They never show any real stuff. They never have girls trying to change their boyfriends into acting different. Or throwing you out on your rear because you made one lousy mistake!"

Hmmm, I thought, staring at the Doritos. *Each serving of chips provides one-and-a-half grams of saturated fat, and each bag contains fifteen servings. That means if I eat an entire bag . . .*

"And look at this dude! All wimpy and weepy, talking about how lost he would be without her. Who talks like that? Dev? You watching? Look at the TV, Dev. Don't you think that's totally unrealistic?"

"Totally," I agreed, looking back up at the screen. "It's impossible to kiss like that and not get lipstick all over your face."

Sean grunted. "I'm not talking about her makeup, Schaub! I'm talking about all this lovey-dovey crap! That dude is about as cool and mysterious as a bar of soap, and he has this total babe throwing herself at him. The real world just doesn't work that way."

All of a sudden something inside me snapped like a potato chip, and a red-hot rage flooded over me.

"I am sick and tired of hearing your garbage!" I shouted, jumping to my feet. "One girl dumps you and you automatically assume there's something wrong with the entire female sex! You and your stupid pact. Here you thought avoiding girls would make us feel better, and look at us! We're moping around watching soap operas like a couple of wusses!"

Sean sat frozen on the couch. His eyes were wide with shock and his mouth hung halfway open, revealing half-eaten Doritos inside. I couldn't stop myself from ranting, though. The words just kept spewing out on their own.

"And let me tell you something else," I continued. "Your pact and your big macho attitude has cost me someone wonderful. Yeah, that's right. A *girl!* I actually met an incredible girl!"

"What?" he shouted.

"You heard me! I didn't tell you because I was afraid of how you might react. But I'm not scared anymore. And because of this dumb pact and because I was trying to act supercool like you, I've totally lost her trust in me!"

Sean sat quietly fuming, his fists clenching and unclenching in his lap. As I looked at him my fury subsided and I only felt sorry for the guy.

"I can't believe you." He glared at me and shook his head. "What a total wimp."

I let out a deep sigh and lowered my voice. "Look, I'm your buddy, Sean, and I hate to see you like this. But you've got to get back to reality, man. You're only making things worse."

"You don't know anything," he said through clenched teeth. "And you're not my buddy. Not anymore."

"I'm sorry," I said, more out of pity than regret. Then I turned and started for the door.

"Yeah, go ahead!" Sean called out. "Run away from me."

As I stepped out into the hallway I paused and looked back. "I'm not running *from* anyone, Sean. I'm running *to* someone."

I was glad I'd remembered to grab my windbreaker on the way out. Either the weather was finally starting to seem more wintry or the chill I felt inside was making me feel cold on the outside. During the long walk down the beach, the turtle box I'd stashed in my front zipper pocket kept thumping against my heart, as if it were trying to tell me something.

When I reached the coffee shop, I looked through the front window for several minutes. I needed some time to get up my nerve. The place was packed, but eventually the throng of people up front cleared out enough to reveal Halle working the cappuccino machine.

What the heck am I going to say to her? I wondered. *What if just the sight of me sends her into another rage and she dumps a whole pot of hot coffee on me? Maybe I should just stay away and spare her—and me—any more pain.*

As I sighed and leaned against the window the ceramic turtle in my pocket knocked against the glass. Another sign? On an impulse I took it out, removed the layers of tissue paper, and studied it.

I was pondering the sly smile on the turtle's face when a voice said, "Man, it's cold out here!"

I nearly jumped through the window. For a split second I thought the turtle was somehow communicating with me. Then I saw Bowman standing nearby, rubbing the tops of his arms where they poked out of his Hawaiian shirt.

"Oh, hey there," I said.

"That's a cool turtle," he remarked, pointing to the box. "Yeah. Turtles are way cool. You know what's really wild about them?"

"No, what?" I asked impatiently, staring through the glass at Halle.

Bowman took a couple of side steps closer to me and said in an ominous voice, "Their shells, man."

Big wow, I thought. *Tell it to your Ouija board.*

"You know, they look all tough because of their shells, but they're not," he went on. "Take its shell off, and a turtle's really kinda small and soft. The shell is just protection, dude. It's not the real thing."

I shot him a confused look, but he just smiled at me, slapped me on the back, and strode into the coffee shop. I didn't know if he was subtly trying to tell me something or just going off on the wondrous biology of a reptile. Either way, Bowman had managed to raise my confidence enough to go face Halle. Sometimes things *do* work in mysterious ways.

"Good afternoon. Can I get you anyth—" Halle froze in midsentence when she looked up from the cash register and saw me.

"Yes, I'd like a second chance, please," I said.

Halle blinked back at me a couple of times, then stared down at the counter. "You're not funny, Devin," she said softly. "Please don't do this." The edge she'd had in her voice the previous day was gone. Now she just seemed hurt.

"I'm serious. Just let me explain some things to you, and then I promise I'll leave you alone." I crouched down a bit so I could look into her downcast eyes. "Please, Halle? Can't you take a quick break?"

"No! Can't you see I'm busy?"

"You go ahead, Halle," Bowman interrupted. "I'll handle things."

"It's too crowded, Bowman. No way."

"Way. I've got it covered. Watch." He pointed to each customer down the line. "Let's see . . . mochaccino, café au lait, double espresso—wait, no—decaf double espresso, strawberry smoothie, and cappuccino with extra foam. Right?"

The customers all stared back at Bowman totally speechless, then nodded in unison.

"See?" he said to Halle. "I got it down. Now

take five and let me work my magic."

He shimmied in beside her and nudged her out of the way, starting on the next order. Halle stood there with a defeated look on her face for a few seconds, then took off her apron and threw it under the counter. "Fine!" she said. "You have five minutes."

She marched through the seating area and sat down at the same small table where we'd played cards five days earlier.

"Well? I'm listening." She crossed her legs, folded her arms across her chest, and lifted her chin defiantly. *Like a turtle hiding in its shell,* I thought.

"I'm sorry—for everything. I've been a total jerk, and I'm sorry I misled you."

She sighed impatiently and raised her eyebrows. "Is that all?"

"No, there's more. Lots more. Just hear me out, okay?"

Taking a deep breath, I launched into the whole story. I told her everything, starting with my catching Tasha with Brad and ending with my lame attempt to see her secretly without telling Sean. Actually, it felt good to let it all out—like I was finally getting around to unpacking after having been there a week. The whole time I talked, Halle sat there staring at me, her head tilted sideways and her large eyes examining me like infrared scanners.

"So that's it?" she asked when I'd finished. "That's everything? You lied for your friend's sake?"

"Yeah. Well . . . partly."

"Go on."

I sighed heavily and twiddled my fingers nervously. "I also saw meeting you as a chance to act more . . . cool. Sean's always telling me that I open up too much with women and that I need to be more mysterious."

"This is the friend who thought up the pact? He sounds messed up."

"I've only recently realized that. Sean's one of those guys girls drool over, and I figured if I acted elusive like him, it might pay off. Sneaking around the way I did seemed to naturally give me that image."

Halle twisted her face into a scowl and stared out the window.

What a loser I am! I thought. I figured that she now hated me even more. But at least she knew the truth. She deserved that.

"I'm really sorry," I said lamely. "I know I blew it, and I don't blame you for not forgiving me."

She continued to gaze contemplatively at the pier outside.

"Well, anyway. Thanks for hearing me out," I said. "Oh, and this is for you." I took the turtle out of my pocket and set it on the table. "I never really got the chance to give it to you."

Still no reaction.

"So . . . bye." This was it. I stopped to take one last long look at her before I left forever. My heart seemed to liquefy as I studied her face—eyes as green and sparkly as a Christmas tree, hair as wavy as the ocean outside, lips as soft as . . . I quickly wrenched my eyes off her and twisted in my chair to go.

"That's ironic," she said suddenly.

"What? What is?" I sat back down and stared at her.

"Here you were changing yourself for me, and the whole time I was sort of changing myself for you." She exhaled heavily, uncrossing her arms and erasing the hostility from her face. "See, I know what it's like not to reveal too much about yourself. That's how I usually am. Only I don't act that way to seem cool—I do it to protect myself. After the whole mess with my mom, dad, and stepdad, I never wanted to get close to someone because I was afraid they'd stomp all over me. You know?"

I nodded.

"My friends and the guys I dated were always telling me to open up more, but I couldn't. Then when I met you, it seemed so easy. I found myself telling you things I normally wouldn't. I don't know why—it just seemed natural. Things clicked with us."

"I know. I felt it too."

For a moment we were silent. Halle picked up the turtle and gazed into its grinning face.

"It's too bad we can't just hit a rewind button and start over again," she said. "Only this time be ourselves from the start."

I opened my mouth to say something but

was interrupted when Bowman yelled from the front counter.

"Hey, Halle! The cash register is, like, beeping really loudly. I think it's mad at me."

"Guess my time's up," she said, rolling her eyes. She stood, paused for a second by my chair, and then raced off to the front.

While she fiddled with the register tape, I snuck into the line at the counter.

"Hi. Sorry about the wait. What can I get you?" Halle asked me as she feverishly punched buttons on the machine and reset it.

"You got any orange juice?" I asked in my best Oklahoma drawl.

Her head jerked up in surprise. "I think I can manage that." She smiled.

"My name's Devin. I'm staying in town a while and was wondering if you'd like to join me for a jog sometime. Here." I grabbed a pen and started to scrawl on a napkin. "This is the number where I'm staying."

"My name's Halle," she said, grasping my hand and shaking it. "And I'd love to."

Seventeen

Sean

THE SODA CAN buckled under the weight of my palms. I twisted the metal and it ripped open, a few renegade drops of cola dripping onto my lap.

How could Devin betray me like that? I thought angrily just as Gary walked in the front door.

"Hey, Scary. I thought you were still sleeping. Did you have to go to work early or something?"

"Sean, I need to talk to you," he said, his tone very serious. "Where's Devin?"

"Who cares?" I muttered angrily. "We had a fight and he ran out of here."

"Oh. I'm sorry. Well, maybe it's better if I tell you this alone." He sat down next to me on the couch and started rubbing his hands together the way he does when he's thinking hard about something.

"What is it, Scary?" The tense look on his face was making me nervous.

"I don't know if you noticed that things are a bit different around here."

Oh, no, I thought, *here it comes.*

"I didn't come home at all last night."

Immediately I feared the worst. "Where were you? Jail? The hospital? Man, I figured something weird was going on with you, but I never thought—"

"No, no. Nothing like that," he said quickly. "I was at my girlfriend's house."

"Girlfriend?"

"Yeah. You've met her—sort of." He gave me a sheepish grin. "Julie? The one I told you was my hired help?"

"She's your girlfriend?"

"Yep. We've been dating for a few months now. Lately it's gotten serious—very serious. In fact, I'm moving in with her at the end of the year. That's why so much of my stuff is gone."

"Why didn't you tell me?" I asked.

"I was going to, but then you called me about Jo Beth and your plan to come out here and recover," Gary explained. "Your mom called soon after you did that day. She told me how you hadn't been yourself for weeks—avoiding friends, avoiding family, and snapping at people all the time."

"Aw, man! That's just Claire making a big deal out of nothing."

"Is it? Since you arrived, you've moped around the condo all day. I'm worried about you, homeboy. I was hoping your pact would work out for you, but you don't seem any better."

"I'm fine! Why does everyone keep telling me I'm not? I just need to give my plan a little more time."

Gary sighed and looked down at his hands. "Look, I know where you're coming from. I'm thirty-seven years old. For years I thought settling down with a woman would rob me of all my powers. But then I met Julie. What we have is special. And instead of feeling trapped or limited, I feel stronger and more at ease. I'm a better person with her."

For the second time that day, I was shocked speechless. I would never have guessed that Gary, of all people, was capable of sounding like a Hallmark card.

"I love her, Sean," he continued. "I don't expect you to understand, but trust me on this. Don't avoid women because of one bad experience. That would be like quitting football because of one bad game."

I couldn't listen to him any longer. I stood up so fast, I thought my knee brace would pop off. Without looking at Gary, I started for the door.

"Sean? You okay? Where're you going?"

"I'm outta here!" I called over my shoulder.

I had to get away before any more mind-blowing news was thrown at me. I needed time to absorb everything that had happened so far.

And for the first time in years, I was afraid I might cry.

There's something about lying on a beach that helps you think. The soft sand adjusts to any position you might be sprawled in, and the pounding of the surf always seems to clear your head.

After splitting from Gary, I walked down the beach a ways, flopped down on the ground, and let all my emotions come busting out. Luckily there were no people nearby to see the tears running down my face—only a flock of gigantic seagulls that circled over me, thinking I might have food. Or maybe they were vultures mistaking *me* for food.

"Go away," I said hoarsely. "I'm still alive."

Or was I? For weeks I'd felt empty and mechanical, like I was just running pass patterns instead of actually competing. The only times I'd really felt alive were when I was with Alex.

Prerecorded voices started to echo in my head. First Claire's, saying, "What are you so afraid of?" Then Gabriel's: "You aren't scared of nothing!" Next Devin's: "You've got to get back to reality, man." And finally Gary's: "Don't avoid women because of one bad experience. That would be like quitting football because of one bad game."

Suddenly everyone's words hit home. They were right. All along I'd been scared—scared of letting someone have power over my feelings again. For years I'd thought of Devin as a wimp, but now I realized that he was the one with the guts to start over again. And Gary . . . I thought of the look on his face when he'd said, "I love her, Sean." The guy was totally happy. Happier than I'd ever seen him.

I was up and running as fast as my knee brace would allow. Sand scattered everywhere and the seagulls squawked in surprise, flying in all directions.

Alex opened her door to find me out of breath and covered with sand. "Sean! What's wrong? Don't tell me it's the dishwasher again."

"No, no. Everything's cool. It's just me. I . . . I need to talk to you."

Her forehead bunched up into a scowl.

"Please, Alex? Can I just come in for a little while?"

"I don't think so." She started to shut the door.

"Wait!" I thrust my hand into the door frame and leaned inside. "Just hear me out, okay? Please? As a good neighbor?"

She sighed heavily. "All right," she said. "But wipe your feet."

As we entered the living room Gabriel's voice sounded from his room down the hall. "Who is it, Alex?"

"No one. Don't worry about it," she yelled back. Then she turned to me. "Let's go talk on the balcony."

I followed her through the French doors and

onto the balcony. For a minute we leaned against the railing facing each other, neither of us saying a word.

"I'm sorry I was such a jerk," I finally blurted out. "I've been really crazy lately. A lot has happened. But now I know what's wrong with me."

The words spilled out at an urgent speed. I sounded like Gabriel whenever he gets excited.

"See, my girlfriend dumped me right before I came to California, and I didn't see it coming. I was so blown away, I decided to avoid girls the whole time I was here so I could get a grip on myself. Then I met you. I—I totally fell for you, and that freaked me out. I was afraid of getting hurt again, so I stayed away. Like you and the roller coasters."

Alex's eyes grew wider by the second. I couldn't tell if she was moved, angry, or weirded out by my rambling confession.

"I tried to tell myself that seeing you wasn't anything serious, but that was just a lame cover." I grasped her hands and slowly pulled her to me. "When we kissed out here that day, I realized I'd been fooling myself. The feelings I had for you were stronger than anything, and that meant losing you would hurt worse than anything, so I cut and ran."

A tear wriggled out of the corner of her eye and perched itself on the curve of her cheekbone. I raised my hand and gently brushed it away with my thumb.

"I'm crazy about you, Alex," I murmured. "I'm not afraid to say it now. You make me feel . . . stronger, like I'm a better person when I'm with you. I—I love you, and I don't want us to give up on each other. That would be like . . . like forfeiting a game because I'm afraid of losing." I knew I sounded like a cheap valentine, but I didn't care.

"I don't want to give up either," she said, her voice soft. "And I was scared too. Scared of loving someone and then losing them—again. That's why I pushed you away."

"But I'm back," I whispered, leaning over and touching my forehead to hers.

"Yes. You are."

We kissed slowly, and I could feel the world all around me going normal again. Or maybe I went normal. In any case, it finally seemed like the game of life was turning in my favor.

"Wait a second," I said, pulling away. "There's something I need to do."

"What? Where are you going?" She watched anxiously as I walked away and started heading back through the balcony doors.

"I need to make a long-distance call—a real one this time."

"To who?"

"To a UCLA scout who gave me his card two months ago. I've just found out where I belong."

Eighteen

Devin

IT WAS LATE in the afternoon. The sun inched toward the watery horizon, stirring up breezes and filling the sky with streaks of orange and lavender. Slowly I headed back to the condo. I was feeling, as Sean would say, totally stoked about having made up with Halle. But each step I took toward Gary's also brought me in closer range of Sean's fists. I was not looking forward to facing him.

Strangely enough, though, I wasn't scared of him. Standing up to him earlier had made me realize that he wasn't a superhuman studly dude. Sure, he was tough, stubborn, and athletic, but he was also as flawed and vulnerable as the rest of us.

He was a really good friend, though, and I needed to make amends. Sean had always looked out for me, and lately all I'd done was lie to him.

I would apologize, but I wouldn't let him tell me what I should or shouldn't do anymore.

As I walked down the hallway to Gary's door I heard laughter coming from inside. I opened the door cautiously.

"Devin! There you are! Come on in!" Gary called. He was sitting on the couch next to a beautiful blond woman. Sean was on the recliner next to them.

"Uh . . . hey, guys," I said, confused. "What's up?"

"I want you to meet someone," Gary said, motioning me over. He stood, grabbed the hand of the woman, and gently pulled her up beside him. "This is Julie, my girlfriend. Well, actually . . . I have to get used to saying this . . . my fiancée."

Then he smiled gigantically, nervously shifting his weight from one foot to the other like a hyperactive kid. Julie looked just as happy but more composed. She held out her hand.

"Nice to meet you," she said.

"Likewise. So . . . you two are engaged?" I was totally blown away. When did all this happen?

"That's right," Julie told me. "Care to check out Gary's Christmas gift to me?" She held up her left hand. A small round diamond sparkled on her fourth finger.

"Wow, Gary! What a surprise!"

He shuffled his feet bashfully and rubbed his hands together. I half expected him to say, "Aw, shucks."

"So . . . why . . . when . . . how come I didn't know about this?" I stammered.

Gary looked pointedly at Sean. "Long story."

"Come sit with us," Julie said. "We were just about to drink a Coca-Cola toast."

I pulled up a dining-room chair while Gary ran to get me a glass. Then we raised our tumblers.

"To the happy couple!" I exclaimed.

"To true love!" Sean added. I was amazed at how well he was taking all this.

We all clinked glasses. Gary and Julie gazed at each other lovingly. I looked at Sean to gauge his reaction, but he was staring down at his drink. It was obvious he didn't want to make eye contact with me.

"Oh! Look at the time!" Gary jumped up. "Julie and I need to be at the restaurant in ten minutes! Sorry to run like this, guys, but we have reservations."

"No problem," Sean said.

Julie shook my hand again and hugged Sean before they left.

Once the door shut and their footsteps died away, Sean looked at me.

"So . . . Uncle Gary's engaged, huh?" I asked lamely.

"Yeah," he said absently, as if he hadn't really heard the question. Then he rose from his chair and began cracking his knuckles.

Here goes, I thought dismally. I stood up to face him.

"Look, Dev, about our fight this morning . . . there are some things that need to get straightened out."

Yeah, like my nose after you've smashed it sideways.

"I just want you to know . . ." He paused and took a deep breath. "I'm sorry, man."

"Huh?" I was so shocked, I almost collapsed back into the chair.

"You were right. The pact was totally dumb. I was just wigging out, I guess."

It was weird to see Sean so humble and awkward.

"You been out seeing that girl of yours?" he asked.

"Yeah."

Sean nodded. "Well, you don't need to sneak around anymore. In fact, I'd like to meet her. So would Gary and Julie. Maybe the six of us could go out sometime."

"Sure. But who's the sixth? Don't you mean five of us?"

Sean smiled, the familiar cockiness returning to his face. "You hungry?" he asked.

"Huh? Yeah, but—"

"Come on," he said, steering me toward the front door. "I know where we can get some killer tamales."

Nineteen

Sean

"TEN . . . NINE . . . EIGHT . . . seven . . . six . . . five . . . four . . . three . . . two . . . one! Happy New Year!" everyone yelled.

"Blastoff!" Gabriel hollered.

Alex and I laughed as we kissed. Next to us Devin planted a big sloppy one on his new girlfriend. That's my boy! The dude found himself a total babe—eyes greener than a Packers' jersey, legs five miles high. And she's cool too. A 'Niners fan, even.

We all sat on a big quilt on the beach near the condo. Gary and Julie had gone to a big ritzy bash at the hotel. They invited us to come along, but Mrs. Lopez was working late at the hospital and Alex had to baby-sit Gabriel. Of course I wanted to be with her, and Devin and Halle were happy to hang with us. The next day Dev and I were flying back to Oklahoma. I couldn't think of a better way to spend my last night in California than holding Alex on a breezy beach.

"Okay, guys. Grab a drink and we'll toast the new year," Alex said. She pulled five plastic cups and a bottle of that fake wine stuff out of the picnic basket. "Who wants to do the toasting honors?"

"I will," Devin offered. Once everyone had their glasses filled and raised, he cleared his throat and said, "To a new year"—he turned and flashed Halle a lovey-dovey look—"and new beginnings."

"Here, here!" we all chimed in.

"Time to turn in now, Gabriel," Alex announced. "I promised you could stay up to ring in the year as long as you went straight to bed afterward, remember?"

"But I'm not sleepy! You guys just want me to go away so you can kiss some more!"

"That's right," I said at the same time that Alex yelled, "That's not true!"

Gabriel gave me a knowing smile. "Okay. I'll go to bed."

"Thanks," I said, reaching over and mussing up his hair. "Come on, I'll walk up with you guys."

Alex hugged Devin good-bye since she probably wouldn't see him again before we left. Then she turned and hugged Halle, making her promise to drop by sometime. I reached out to shake Halle's hand, but she threw her arms around me in an embrace.

"It's great to finally meet you," she exclaimed. "Remember to cheer our guys to a Super Bowl victory."

"You got it."

Alex and I headed back to the condo, carrying the picnic basket between us, while Gabriel ran in front, talking the whole way.

"So, when you go to UCLA and play on the football team, does that mean you can get me tickets?"

"Of course. Although we don't know for sure yet if I'll get in."

"Sure, you will. You said that guy was sending a letter. And Alex is going to UCLA too."

"Gabriel, I haven't been accepted yet."

"You will. 'Cause you're supersmart. You get all A's all the time and you scored fifteen thousand on the SAT."

"Fifteen *hundred,* Gabriel." Alex laughed as we stepped onto the elevator.

"Well, anyhow. You guys are both going to UCLA. I know it."

"How can you be so sure?" I asked.

"I don't know. I just feel it. Maybe I'm psycho."

"*Psychic,* Gabriel," Alex corrected him. "Psycho means you're crazy—well, maybe you're that too."

We stepped off the elevator and trudged down the corridor to their condo.

"All right, Psychic-man. Say good-bye to Sean and then time for bed." Alex gestured to Gabriel's room.

"Wait," I interrupted. "Before you go, Gabriel, I have a present for you. Sort of a late Christmas gift."

"Really? What is it?" he asked, his tired eyes widening.

I pulled a small, thin rectangle from my pocket, wrapped in blue Kleenex. "Open it and see."

Gabriel tore open the tissue and held the card in his hand. "Oh, wow!" he hollered. "Your lucky Jerry Rice! Thanks!"

He reached up and hugged me fiercely. I was surprised at how strong the little dude was.

"You're welcome," I said.

"Don't worry. I'll take good care of it," he said solemnly. "I'm going to go add it to my collection right now. Good-bye! See ya soon!"

"Good night, Gabriel."

I watched him race off to his room and shut the door. Then I turned to find Alex staring at me. She was smiling, but her eyes were all misty looking.

"That was really sweet," she said. "But are you sure you want to give him that? It's your lucky charm."

"I don't need it anymore. I already have everything I've ever wanted." I reached out and wrapped her in my arms. "Gabriel's right about everything working out for us. I feel it too."

"So do I," she murmured, her lips closing in on mine. "After all, like Devin said, it's our year."

Devin

After Sean, Alex, and Gabriel left, Halle suggested we go for a stroll on the beach. Tiny pinpricks of lights surrounded us: the stars in the sky, the lights of the buildings, and the reflections of it all shimmering in the water below.

"I like him," Halle said. "I didn't expect to, after everything you told me, but Sean seems like a great guy."

"He is. And Alex seems really good for him."

We stopped walking and faced the rolling waves. I stood behind Halle and draped my arms around her, inhaling the crisp, salty air. It was amazing what could happen in two weeks: I'd stood up to Sean for the first time. Sean dropped the macho attitude and found someone special. And I had fallen for a beautiful girl with a tattoo and brand-new gold hoop through her nostril. California—you gotta love it!

"I can't believe you're leaving tomorrow," she said as we swayed back and forth to the rhythm of the crashing waves.

"Just for a few months. I'll be back this summer for Gary and Julie's wedding."

"I can't wait. I bet you look incredibly *GQ* in a tux."

"You know," I whispered, letting my chin rest on her shoulder, "you could always come see me in Oklahoma over spring break. We have plenty of fine state universities you could check out. I bet you could find one with an excellent restaurant management school."

She swiveled in my arms to face me. "Sure, but what about a track team? How well do people run out there?"

"Like the wind sweeping down the plains."

Halle smiled. She looked so beautiful in the moonlight, I stroked her cheeks and ran my fingers through her hair just to make certain she was real.

"So, you never told me what your perfect moment ended up being," she said.

"Actually, it hasn't happened yet," I replied, inching my face closer to hers. "But it's about to." Then, with the waves lapping gently behind us and amateur fireworks lighting up the sky, we kissed. And the whole world, for a brief, wonderful instant, was truly perfect.

Jenny and Jake Love Quiz:

Are You Ready for Love?

We're all in love with the idea of being in love, and why not? It's easy to be tempted by the thought of a soul mate who understands you completely and will always be there for you. But love isn't easy, and relationships take hard work. Take Jenny and Jake's love quiz to see if you're ready for the real thing or still attached to the single life.

1. *You went through the "boys are gross" stage:*

   a. Too long ago to remember
   b. A couple of years back
   c. It's a stage?

2. *A perfect kiss is most like:*

   a. Sinking into a tingly yet soothing bubble bath
   b. Snuggling into bed and wrapping your most comfy blanket around you
   c. Soaring down on the new roller coaster at Disney World

3. *You spot a gorgeous guy moving in with his family across the street from you. Your first thought:*

   a. I hope his face looks as nice close up as it does far away.
   b. I hope his personality is as nice as his eyes are.
   c. I hope he's as nice to me as he's being to his mother right now.

4. *Let's play the word-association game. I say* commitment *and you say:*

   a. *Aargh!*
   b. Mmmm . . .
   c. Huh?

5. *A cozy night at home with your boyfriend, a video, and some pizza sounds:*

   a. Perfect—some time alone together!
   b. Great—once in a while.
   c. Boring—isn't that what your parents do?

6. *Your dating history most resembles America's history in:*

   a. 1776—a clean slate
   b. 1800s—a few battles
   c. 1998—a couple of world wars, major scars

7. *Your best friend tells you she's swearing off guys—they're no good. Your reaction:*

   a. She's so wrong! She *has* had some rotten luck, but she needs to realize that bitterness isn't the answer.
   b. She's so right! You can't trust any of them.
   c. She's so confused! You've been hurt too, but that doesn't mean that plenty of guys aren't trustworthy.

8. *Remember the word-association game? It's time for a little vocabulary quiz.* Exclusive *means:*

   a. You can't date anyone else—unless he's really, *really* cute.
   b. Other guys are off-limits. Period.
   c. Death! The end of your freedom and liberty!

9. *Your favorite way to spend free time is:*

a. Hanging out with friends, meeting people, being social
b. One-on-one time with the people you care most about
c. Free time? What's that? Every waking minute goes to your schoolwork and planning for the future.

10. *Your boyfriend's best friend is incredibly hot, and you used to have a little crush on him. At a party you end up alone together. How would you act?*

a. You'd be babbling your butt off to hide your overwhelming desire to kiss him.
b. You'd be totally comfortable with him since you know he's not the one you want.
c. You'd try to ignore his beautiful green eyes and remind yourself that you're in love with his best friend.

11. *Not every relationship lasts forever. If you and your boyfriend realize things aren't meant to be, you would:*

a. Cry, rally your friends around you, eat some Hershey's, then try to move on

b. Cry, push everyone away from you, eat everything in sight, then move to another country

c. Cry, snap at a few friends, eat a pint of Ben & Jerry's, then move away from dating for a while

Turn the page to find out your score!

Scoring:

1.	(a) 3	(b) 2	(c) 1
2.	(a) 2	(b) 3	(c) 1
3.	(a) 1	(b) 2	(c) 3
4.	(a) 1	(b) 3	(c) 2
5.	(a) 3	(b) 2	(c) 1
6.	(a) 1	(b) 3	(c) 2
7.	(a) 2	(b) 1	(c) 3
8.	(a) 2	(b) 3	(c) 1
9.	(a) 2	(b) 3	(c) 1
10.	(a) 1	(b) 3	(c) 2
11.	(a) 3	(b) 1	(c) 2

If you scored between 11 and 18:

Okay, here's the blunt truth: You're not ready to be tied down. Maybe you feel like you need to spend your time on other things, or you want the option of going out with that cute guy in biology, or you just haven't had enough experience with dating to be able to handle the tougher moments and the possibility of a broken heart. It's okay if an intense relationship isn't for you right now—give yourself time, and don't commit until you're sure it's right.

If you scored between 19 and 25:

You're on the fence about this one, right? In some ways you couldn't be more thrilled over the idea of a significant other, but you have a couple of doubts or you're just not *quite* there yet. The best thing to do is to go over this quiz and check out which questions made you hesitate. This will clue you in on what still needs to change. You're certainly on the right track if love is what you're looking for, but it's best not to get involved until you're sure you understand exactly what you want from a relationship.

If you scored between 26 and 33:

Being in love is exciting and fun, but it also takes work, time, and maturity—and that's old news to you. You've been through enough to know the deal, and commitment looks good. Just remember that being ready doesn't mean the perfect guy will magically appear before you—love's about timing too. But once you do find a guy who's equally primed for true love and totally right for you, go for it!

Do you ever wonder about falling in love? About members of the opposite sex? Do you need a little friendly advice but have no one to turn to? Well, that's where we come in . . . Jenny and Jake. Send us those questions you're dying to ask, and we'll give you the straight scoop on life and love in the nineties.

DEAR JAKE

Q: *When I first met Matt, he seemed like the greatest guy ever. And he is really cool, but now I know that he's not right for me. How can I break this to him when I was the one who originally convinced him we should go out?*

DW, San Diego, CA

A: Ouch. Not only will he be hurt, he'll resent you for reeling him in only to toss him back into the sea. That's your fear, right? It doesn't have to be this bad, though. No matter what, Matt will not greet this news with joy. But it sounds like you do still care about him even though you've realized romance isn't in the cards. So handle the situation with honesty and sensitivity, letting him know that your opinion of him hasn't changed just because you realize you two aren't meant to be. Maybe Matt will even come to the same realization, and you'll move painlessly into a friendship.

Q: *My boyfriend, Jordan, has been acting really strange lately. He used to treat me so well, but now he ignores me all the time and doesn't talk much when I call him. I asked him if he wanted to break up and he said no, but it seems like we might as well not be going out. What's going on?*

LA, Charlotte, NC

A: It's possible that Jordan is going through a hard time in some other area of his life, like in school or at home, and he needs time alone. Maybe he doesn't want to lay his problems on you and figures he should just deal with it on his own and then come back to you when things are better. Do you know of any conflicts he's been having with his parents or any classes he's struggling in?

If it seems like the rest of his life is just fine, then unfortunately your suspicions could be correct. A lot of wimpy guys are afraid to tell their girlfriends directly that they want out because they're scared of confrontation. Jordan could be sending you signals with the hope that you'll get the message and quietly disappear. Don't let him get away with this—instead of asking him if he wants to break up, tell him that you're sick of him treating you like this and you need a straight answer about what's up. If he won't explain and things don't improve, it's time to tell him good-bye.

DEAR JENNY

Q: *My boyfriend's ex-girlfriend and I get along really well. It's strange, I know, but we just have a lot in common. The problem is that my boyfriend, Roger, is very uncomfortable with me and Jamie being friends. I guess he's afraid that we'll talk about him or something. How can I get him to accept my friendship with Jamie?*

MB, Austin, TX

A: How would you feel if Roger was hanging out with one of your exes? Think about it for a second, and then maybe you'll understand where he's coming from. Did he and Jamie have a bad breakup? Perhaps it's not the friendship that upsets him as much as the fact that he has to keep being around someone he's trying to move on from. You certainly have a right to choose your own friends, and if Jamie means a lot to you, Roger shouldn't ask you to give that up. However, you could try to be more sensitive about his feelings and refrain from talking about Jamie with him, or make sure that you hang with her on nights when he's busy somewhere else. I think that as long as your friendship isn't being thrown in his face all the time, he'll learn to deal with it.

Q: *I overheard some guys talking about the kind of girls they like, and I don't fit the description at all. What does this mean?*

PW, Grenada, MS

A: What it means is that you probably won't ever go out with those guys. Actually, it doesn't even mean that—try making a list of everything you want in a guy, and then compare the list to the guys you've dated. Notice any differences? I read many letters from girls who want to know how they should change to win the guys of their dreams, and the answer I give is always the same—don't. If you try to be someone you're not, you'll never be happy with yourself or with the guy who's with you for false reasons. There is definitely someone out there who has always been looking for everything that you are, and don't give up until you find him.

Do you have questions about love? Write to:
Jenny Burgess or Jake Korman
c/o Daniel Weiss Associates
33 West 17th Street
New York, NY 10011

Don't miss any of the books in Love Stories
—the romantic series from Bantam Books!

#1 *My First Love* . . . . Callie West
#2 *Sharing Sam* . . . . Katherine Applegate
#3 *How to Kiss a Guy* . . . . Elizabeth Bernard
#4 *The Boy Next Door* . . . . Janet Quin-Harkin
#5 *The Day I Met Him* . . . . Catherine Clark
#6 *Love Changes Everything* . . . . ArLynn Presser
#7 *More Than a Friend* . . . . Elizabeth Winfrey
#8 *The Language of Love* . . . . Kate Emburg
#9 *My So-called Boyfriend* . . . . Elizabeth Winfrey
#10 *It Had to Be You* . . . . Stephanie Doyon
#11 *Some Girls Do* . . . . Dahlia Kosinski
#12 *Hot Summer Nights* . . . . Elizabeth Chandler
#13 *Who Do You Love?* . . . . Janet Quin-Harkin
#14 *Three-Guy Weekend* . . . . Alexis Page
#15 *Never Tell Ben* . . . . .Diane Namm
#16 *Together Forever* . . . . .Cameron Dokey
#17 *Up All Night* . . . . .Karen Michaels
#18 *24/7* . . . . Amy S. Wilensky
#19 *It's a Prom Thing* . . . . Diane Schwemm
#20 *The Guy I Left Behind* . . . . Ali Brooke
#21 *He's Not What You Think* . . . . Randi Reisfeld
#22 *A Kiss Between Friends* . . . . Erin Haft
#23 *The Rumor About Julia* . . . . Stephanie Sinclair
#24 *Don't Say Good-bye* . . . . .Diane Schwemm
#25 *Crushing on You* . . . . Wendy Loggia
#26 *Our Secret Love* . . . . Miranda Harry
#27 *Trust Me* . . . . Kieran Scott
#28 *He's the One* . . . . Nina Alexander
#29 *Kiss and Tell* . . . . Kieran Scott
#30 *Falling for Ryan* . . . . Julie Taylor
#31 *Hard to Resist* . . . . Wendy Loggia
#32 *At First Sight* . . . . Elizabeth Chandler

Super Editions

Listen to My Heart . . . . Katherine Applegate
Kissing Caroline . . . . Cheryl Zach
It's Different for Guys . . . . Stephanie Leighton
My Best Friend's Girlfriend . . . . Wendy Loggia
Love Happens . . . . Elizabeth Chandler
Out of My League . . . . Everett Owens
A Song for Caitlin . . . . J. E. Bright
The "L" Word . . . . Lynn Mason

Coming soon:

#33 *What We Did Last Summer* . . . . . . Elizabeth Craft

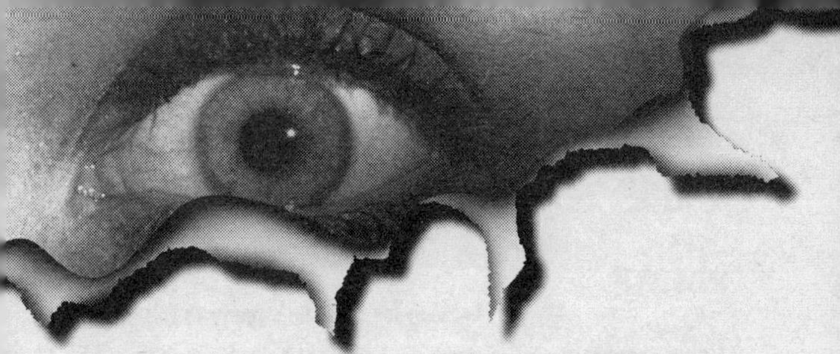

You'll always remember your first love.

Looking for signs he's ready to fall in love?
Want the guy's point of view?
Then you should check out the Love Stories series.
Romantic stories that tell it like it is—why he doesn't call, how to ask him out, when to say good-bye.

The Love Stories series is available at a bookstore near you.